The Medlar Tree

To Richard Corney

The Medlar Tree

GLENDA BEAGAN

SEREN BOOKS

SEREN BOOKS is the book imprint of
Poetry Wales Press Ltd
Andmar House, Tondu Road, Bridgend, Mid Glamorgan

ISBN 1-85411-068-3

Cover illustration by Rhianedd Thomas

The publisher acknowledges the financial assistance of the
Welsh Arts Council

Printed in 11 point Palatino
by The Cromwell Press, Melksham

Contents

The Sea Book

It was like a young shark. Lithe, streamlined, with a fierce face.
'What is it?' Gavin asked.
'I dunno,' said Heather.
'It'll die if it stays there.'
'No it won't, stupid. When the tide comes in it'll swim off, won't it?'
'But it's going to get worn out. It's going to hurt itself. Look.'
And she looked. Despite herself. Wrinkling up her face as the creature lashed and fought against the rock. The air was full of the sharp crack of its tail and arching back. She wanted to close her eyes. Get away from here. The shallow water trapping it in the pool, the crack between the layered slabs, seemed to sting, to burn with its fury.
'We'll have to save it.'
'How?'
She heard the sound of her voice become hard, contemptuous. She heard the sneer in it. Why did she have to put up with him all the time? Drag him around everywhere? This place was boring now. She didn't see why she had to come here at all. Why wouldn't they let her go and stay with Claire and Miriam in Guildford?
'I'm going to try and save it.'
'It'll bite you. You'll fall in or something and they'll blame me. Why can't you leave things alone?'
Gavin wasn't listening. He was crouched down on the rocks staring hard at the fish thing as it writhed.
'I just wish we could tell it to wait. To be quiet and wait for the tide.'
'That's what I said. But it's stupid isn't it? It's like you. It hasn't got a brain.'

7

Again he ignored her. It was difficult to get a foothold near enough, among all the weed. Bladderwrack with its blobs for popping. Slithery thongweed. Where could he grip? By the tail? It was big though, wasn't it? And slippery. And it wasn't in the best of tempers.

He'd thought it out. You could tell. Heather wanted to walk away. Leave him. But she couldn't. There he was, like a Red Indian or something, crouched there. Oblivious of her. Oblivious of everything. And she knew, deep down inside, that Gavin was simply better than she was. He was different, yes, but it was more than that. More than their mother would allow. She always said they were chalk and cheese and made a joke about it. But it wasn't funny. At all.

Around them the sea, the sky, the sounds of the estuary. Oystercatchers making their tinny cry. Was it a sad cry? Was it happy? She couldn't decide. Anymore than she could decide whether the lighthouse on its thin, and from here almost invisible, island was something she loved or hated. She turned back to him. She wanted to say something spiteful. But she couldn't. In a horrible way, she knew Gavin was good. Simply good. And knowing that made her feel small and mean inside.

'I've got him.'

Gavin's shout, Gavin's running, was everywhere. The whole place, the rocks, the clouds, the air, was full of Gavin. And the fish thing, that was Gavin too, as he went hurtling off over the glittering wet stones of the promontory, with it wriggling, fighting in his grip. Almost slipping, almost flat on his face, but catching himself as he started to fall, swivelling back upright, then on again, until, just at the point where the stones filtered out, and the deep channel of the river, narrow and deep, a dark green, almost black, reached the sea, he stopped, raising both hands with the great slippery fish thing between them, and flung. And as the fish hit the water there was a sound like a door slamming, or a gun going off. A sideways, steady fling, with hardly a splash, so the fish joined the current at just the right angle, in just the right place.

'You should've seen it,' he said, catching up with her, breathless, as she picked her way back. 'It was brilliant. Just like it was flying.'

And it wasn't as if he was showing off or anything. He wasn't like that. He just wanted to share it with her. 'Great,' she said, struggling. And then he was off again, running back to the house, past the upturned boats pulled high up on the sandy bit.

* * * * *

It was Heather answered the phone. It didn't matter who answered it. It shouldn't have mattered. But it did. It was Mrs Evans, and she asked to speak to Dr Penry, so Heather knew something was wrong. Mrs Evans had only phoned once before and that was after the gales, when the big ash tree had fallen and smashed the greenhouse. There weren't many tall trees on Anglesey, she'd said, as if in some way having a tall tree was wrong. This was worse, though. Heather just knew. You could tell by her voice.

'He's not in at the moment,' Heather said. 'Can I give him a message?'

'Is your mother there, dear?'

'Yes. I'll get her.'

Afterwards they sat in stunned silence. Heather couldn't stand it. Especially the look on Gavin's face.

'It's all my fault,' she said at last, gulping it out, her fingers over her mouth like a claw.

'What on earth makes you think that? Darling, I know you're upset, but really....'

'It is my fault. It's because of me. I didn't want to go last time, did I? I wanted to stay with Claire and Miriam.'

'But that hasn't got anything to do with it. You surely don't think it has....'

Then Gavin started to charge round the room. 'I'll kill them,' he said. 'I'll strangle them with my bare hands. I will. I'll get them. I'll find out where they live and I'll burn their houses down.'

'Now that's enough, the pair of you. Really. This doesn't help. We don't know the extent of the damage yet. It may not be that bad. And you can be sure your father's got the place insured properly.'

Gavin stared open-mouthed at his mother. 'That's not the point. Whether it's insured or not. You just don't understand, do you? You make me sick. If they had to burn somewhere I wish they'd burnt this place. I hate it. Llwyn Onn was my great grandfather's house.'

'I do know that Gavin. I don't think you need to tell me the family history.'

'But you're not a Penry, are you?'

'No, but I am your mother and I won't be spoken to like that.'

'Stop it. For God's sake stop it,' said Heather. 'This is terrible. I wish Daddy was here.'

'So do I. Now just sit down, Gavin. No, better than that, go and make us all a cup of tea. And you can put a drop of whisky in it. For all of us. Yes, for medicinal purposes. And if you think you're old enough to take up the cudgels over matters of family honour, you're old enough to start behaving with a modicum of realism and common sense. And that's a Mainstone speaking. And you can stop looking at me like that.'

Gavin glowered and stormed off to the kitchen. Heather just sat there. Squirming. Listening to the tea things being thumped and banged around. This wasn't how Gavin behaved. She was supposed to be the one with the temper. Everything had been turned upside down.

What did it look like? The house? She saw what Mr Evans must have seen when he got up to see why the dog was barking. She saw the roof of Llwyn Onn ablaze, and then her eyes seemed to sink down through the flames and the smoke, right down to the lean-to at the back. Gavin's den, where he kept all his things. Hers too, since she'd told him she'd grown out of all those old jigsaws and board games. They'd kept them amused when it rained, yes, but he could have them now. It was babyish to want them at all, to still be interested.

And then she saw The Sea Book. Little pink flames like cats' tongues were licking the covers, mended with sticky tape, the spine split right through and glued and glued again. It had belonged to their father, and his before that. Gavin loved it. He'd only been small when he'd discovered it, calling it The Hairloom, pronouncing the 'H' very grandly and deliberately, making them laugh.

She thought of that last day on the shore, the day he'd saved the fish. Then she saw him sat in the den's one huge chair, the book on his knee. He was just like a wizard poring over his spells. 'Here it is,' he said, 'Look, I've got it. It's a lesser spotted dogfish. This is it, exactly. Like a small shark. That's what it says.' And he'd looked up at her, all eagerness. And she'd frozen him out. Like she always did. And it wasn't as if she wanted to do it. She didn't. It made her feel hellish. But she did it just the same.

Why did she feel like this? About Gavin. About Llwyn Onn. The things, the people who meant the most to her. Why did she treat them so badly? It was like a judgement, this burning. Somehow it would have helped to think there really was a God up there, and that this was a punishment. Gavin came into the room carrying the tray. He put it down on the coffee table. Very quietly. Around his mouth the skin was tight and pale. Heather looked at her mother. Couldn't she see it? Didn't she care?

'Get the whisky please, Gavin,' she said.

It was just like watching a play. Gavin brought the decanter from the bureau. Slowly, theatrically, he poured a little whisky into each steaming cup. It was ridiculous. Heather wanted to laugh. Or cry. Or scream. Do something. Didn't dare. And it wasn't just the burning of the house. All this. Whatever it was that was happening.

* * * * *

'Are you sure you want to go over now? It's not going to be too upsetting for you, is it? I wouldn't want that, not after telling your father I'd look after you here. And Elfed says it's not a pretty sight.'

'Gavin's gone Mrs Evans. I don't know why I should have to stay. They didn't want me to come at all but I said it would be worse not seeing.'

'Well there is that. Yes. Imagining things is worse sometimes. But I think it's a pity your mother isn't here with you, myself.'

'She can't be here. She's got a preview at the gallery.'

'Well, maybe, but I still say she should have come. I told her on the phone it can't be anyone local. She mustn't think that, I said. Local people know quite well who your father is. And there's many remember how your grandfather, when he started off, worked with old Dr Lloyd-Jones in Amlwch. Elfed's got a cousin in an old people's home in Llangefni swears it was your great-grandfather loaned them money in the twenties. When times were very bad. Speaks very highly of him. And I've never heard a word said against any of you. Not one. So I told Mrs Penry, I said, you mustn't think badly of us. No one local wanted this to happen.'

'No,' said Heather. 'Anyway, I want to see for myself.'

She left Mrs Evans hovering in the door and walked the long way round. Heavy rain overnight had left deep puddles in the lane. Yellow leaves were floating. And as she turned by the hedge the gable end of Llwyn Onn reared up, looking strangely normal. From this angle it was all a bad joke. Nothing seemed to have happened. Then the front of the house.

Roof fallen in. Charred rafters. The bones of a dinosaur. Black round the windows, smudged against whitewash. Weird. The face of their toy panda on guard in their den. Sat in the big chair. But she'd felt it all when the phone call came. Seen it too. The cats' tongue flames. This was cold somehow. Cold and unreal.

Voices inside. Mr Evans. Her father. No sign of Gavin, but she knew where he'd be.

Past the moored boats. Everything shining. The peeling paint, the sand with glints in it. Crushed shells. Silence. Almost. Just the swishing sound of waves far away. A mist offshore. Hiding the island, the lighthouse. Then the sharp sound of feet on the rocks. Gavin running, carrying something.

'Wait,' she shouted.

But he couldn't hear. Wouldn't have stopped anyway. Looking so small against the bowl of the sky. I'm sorry, she told herself, Sorry for everything, Gavin. I don't mean the things I say. Mostly.

He was standing where he'd stood on the day of the dogfish. In just the same place. And she knew what he was doing. And why. Though there weren't any words to explain.

He paused for a moment, then threw it. What was left of it. Calm.

Strong. The right thing to do. And she watched, strangely comforted, walking slowly towards him over the weed.

The Saddist

He were squirming. He were. He were coming straight for me.'

There is an austere pleasure to be found in porcelain and scouring powder, the clean smell, the grittiness. Not for Mrs Mossop those new-fangled detergent creams. She prefers the old-fashioned stuff, the kind that requires the liberal application of elbow grease. Mine. Hovering explosively at the door she is determined that nothing will divert her narrative flow. The bath needs cleaning, yes, but not as much as her story needs telling.

'He were huge. HUGE. At least a foot long. And in all that rain he were swimming up the path. You should've seen him.'

Swimming. Squirming. I practise my Buddhist detachment. I observe my right arm describe a circle on the pitted surface. Now I concentrate on the stained patches under the taps. Nothing will stop her. She prods me on the shoulder, insistent, and then with an arthritic creak she half-kneels beside me.

'Are you listening? I'm telling you.'

I stop. I must. There is no other way. I stand up, wipe the sweat off my face. How humid it is. Last night's rain, torrential, hours of it. And now this heat. This stuffy little house. Jungle weather.

'He were horrible.'

She pauses, gratified. She now has my full attention.

'Was he an eel or something?'

'Don't know what he were. Like a long worm. Thick, inches of him. And he were squirming.'

So am I. So is she. She is upright again, clutching my hand, pushing her face into mine.

'I were cruel,' she says her voice suddenly fading. And I realise she is afraid and not of the worm, the eel, whatever it was. Of something else. There is a strange hush in the bathroom, broken

for a moment by ice-cream chimes far away.
'I'm a saddist.'
It sounds worse said like that. Absurd. Incongruous. The look on her face. What can I make of it? Relish. Fear. Pride. Shame. A medley. A darkness.
'What did you do?'
I sit on the side of the bath, my face assuming a mask, of what, tolerance, acceptance? What will she say?
'Come and have a look. Come on. In the kitchen.'
I follow, across the boxy hall with its scrap of rug. Orange green swirls.
'Here.'
She stops, pointing at the door into her small square garden. It's open, propped back with a stone.
'Look.'
I look. Nothing. Only the path, the clothes line, two towels and a puce-coloured blouse. The dust bin, the hedge. Beyond it the church tower, the new weather-vane, a gilded fish. It isn't spinning today. The scene is static. The air is static.
'He were there.'
We stand at the door now, looking out at the blandness. It doesn't match. I half expect a monster to materialise before me. Perhaps it has.
'It were the rain,' she says, 'It were hammering. Something in it. He were horrible and I couldn't stand it.' She looks up at me. 'I couldn't.' She has a fine sense of theatre, has Mrs Mossop.
'So what did you do?'
'I got the salt.'
She moves over the cupboard. Stuck on with browned curling sellotape are postcards. Ibiza. Weston-super-Mare. She opens the door. Among cans and soup packets a large earthenware pot. She gets it out, holds it, large eyed, as if cradling Aladdin's lamp.
'This.'
She pokes it under my nose.
'Look.'
I do. 'There's hardly any left.'
'No. I used it all. It were nearly full. On him. To stop him squirming. Stop him coming into the house. 'Cos he were coming. Definite. Coming straight for me.'

I gulp.

'I kept pouring it on him. Out there.'

She nods towards the door. Grimaces. Half shuts her eyes. I see it all now. The rain, the darkness, Mrs Mossop in her pom-pom slippers, a huddled form, the thing on the path in the light from the door. And then the salt. Scooped out. Handful after handful. Then poured. Then panic.

'He were squirming like a mad thing so I kept piling it on him. But it were raining, of course, so it kept melting.'

'Melting?'

'Yes, like a steam were coming off him.'

She rubs her fingernail on the rim of the pot. Finds a crusted bit. Scratches at it.

'Then he stopped squirming. Now she's sat herself on the straight-backed chair by the cooker.

'He were really dead. I checked. I poked him with a stick. There was mountains of salt on him.'

She shudders. 'My sister always said...'

'What?'

'That I were cruel.'

I'm supposed to be cleaning. I haven't even finished the bathroom yet and I'm supposed to be at Mrs Sellingham's by three o'clock. What is all this? Is it real? Another of Mrs Mossop's stalling devices? Always a new story, a new snatch of gossip. But this time it's different.

'She said I were cruel. And I were. I used to kill things. Not just in the house, like a wasp or something. No. Outside too. Things that weren't doing me no harm at all.'

A pause. 'What sort of things?'

'All sorts of things. Ladybirds. Butterflies. Things you're supposed to like. I used to catch the butterflies on the bush by Miss Webb's wall. She were the teacher. I took some to school in a jar one day. She didn't know where from. Put them on her nature table. I drew them in my book after. Red Admirals she said they were.'

She is far away. How many years? Sixty? Seventy?

'And I *mean* kill 'em. Not just let them die. Slowly. Like I said I'm a saddist.' It's very quiet here. No traffic. No ice-cream chimes. Nothing. The last in a row of boxy little houses under the church at the edge of town. She sniffs.

'But it weren't just insects.'

'No?'

'No. When I were married, not long married, I mean the second time, 'cos, my first husband, Cyril, he left, we moved into the new council houses. Nice big houses they were too, but the garden was just meadow, you understand. Never been anything grown there, so Bert dug it all out and planted potatoes to start it off. He worked that hard, he did. Kept a lovely garden.'

'Yes?'

'And I were helping him clear it out one day, down in the long grass and it were damp at the far end. And we had a bonfire for all the dried stuff we'd cleared out before. When I found him.'

'What?'

'A bullfrog. He were a whopper. Like one of them dinosaurs. And I got him on my spade and I were going to chuck him in the fire.'

She clutches the salt pot tighter.

'Bert grabbed the spade off me. He were shocked. You could tell. He said, Lily, you weren't going to burn 'im? Not really? And I said, No.Course not. But I were. I were that ashamed after, the way Bert looked at me. As if he couldn't stand the sight of me. He took that frog down to the pond on the other side of the railway. And I felt he were never the same with me after that. Never.'

She rubs the top button on her cardigan. Baby-blue wool. Pearl button. I glance at my watch surreptitiously. She notices.

'You got to go in a minute?'

'Yes. And I haven't finished the bathroom yet.'

'Never mind. You go to that Mrs Sellingham's after me?'

I nod. A flicker of interest. A wash of change.

'What's she like?'

What do I say? I hover. Suddenly I want to put my arms round Mrs Mossop, hug her, tell her she's not a sadist. That there are all kinds of cruelty in the world and among the many cruelties hers are very small indeed. I could tell her about Mrs Sellingham, couldn't I? The perfect lady in her big house with the stained glass and the fanlight. I don't. I pat her on the hand. Mutter something conciliatory. Pointless.

She sits there. Stares hard at the pans on the shelf.

'Last week it were the snails. On the path that comes down from the precinct, past that big carpet place. There was hundreds of them. I crunched them. I were wearing my new shoes, the ones that pinch, and I went stamping on them, slithering them. Like a jelly all over the path.'

I reach for my coat, thinly, as if trying not to move, to go.

'I don't know why I do it.' She looks me straight in the eye. 'I don't want to be cruel. But I always have been. Always.'

'We all are sometimes,' I say feebly. 'And anyway, there are lots of people who are cruel all the time, much more cruel than you, and they don't even know they're doing it.'

'I know I'm doing it.'

I take the salt pot from her, put it back in the cupboard.

Woman in an Orchard

Listen to the rain. I lie in bed and listen. There is sleet in it. The east wind drives it up alleys, into clogged yards, across the railway sidings.

Yes, there's a whine in the wind and the rain sounds sad. But it's tame rain here somehow. Compared to Nant y Ceiri. I'm glad I lived there, even if it did give Danny a taste of a whole new world beyond me and the kids and, well, other women. I was pretty washed out, wasn't I? Hardly likely to keep up with him. His new life, his new self.

So Nant y Ceiri brought me back. Indirectly. And the kids. How much do they remember? I get the album out, show them the photographs of The Big Snow, when nothing moved in the whole of West Wales but the occasional emergency helicopter. Drifts on the Withybush road behind us were twenty feet deep.

I wish I'd had my camera with me when I saw the bullfinches. They were pecking in the snow, six or seven of them. The deep pink of their breasts like flares in the whiteness, thick chasms of snow, powdery soft or hardpacked like plates of ice. When I think of Nant y Ceiri I think of things like that. Colour. Contrast. The green woodpeckers laughing across the valley. The raven up in the cliffs, calling to his mate with a clear honeyed note like a bell in warm air. The blue hydrangeas, loving the acid soil, the blooms wide as dinner plates.

And I don't feel bitter. About losing Danny I mean. We'd gone as far as we could.

Still, I'm listening to the rain. It was different at Nant y Ceiri. Wilder. Fiercer. Even wetter, I'd say, though that sounds stupid. And I remember lying there in our bed with the great sag in it like a hammock, being pushed up against Danny's back, and thinking

19

of that poor dog up at Prosser's. It had a bit of shelter, I suppose, alongside those old railway carriages where he stored all that stuff. Higgledy-piggledy chaos. What a weird place it was. And him, with his streaky grey black beard like a prophet or something. I used to hear him yell to one of those sons of his across the top field where he kept his small prize flock. Beulahs. Special, he told me. Prosser's Beulahs are famous. They were pretty sheep with handsome striped faces.

But that dog looked so miserable. It wasn't a sheepdog or a guard dog, and stuck out there in the yard in all weathers it certainly wasn't a pet. The first time I saw it Danny'd just driven us up to the Pistyll bend, so he could turn round there, and drive back down the hill, parking more easily against our back wall. That was one bad thing about the cottage. We could only pull up at the side of the road and hope nobody'd try to overtake on the bend and smash into us.

Prosser's was right at the top of the hill, opposite the turning, the name, inscribed in fancy Gothic script on the wall of the house: *D.T. Prosser and Sons, Furnishers. Antique and Contemporary Regular Auctions.*

What a place to find stuck on a bleak hill in the middle of nowhere. To find anywhere, if it comes to that — the house itself, with its pointed gables, its flagpoles and those funny squat little sheds with their shiny black bitumen roofs and twisty chimneys, the cowls like the hoods on old oil lamps. And then there were the railway carriages crammed with bedsteads and rolls of carpet remnants, wardrobes and kitchen cabinets. And the dog, poor thing, sat alongside. It must've been some sort of spaniel cross, with its curly gingery coat, its long ears like a King Charles and the most mournful expression you've ever seen.

I knew nothing about Mr Prosser then and what I did get to know was all hearsay. I try to take as I find and he always treated me kindly, giving us a lift up the hill sometimes, me and the kids, on the way back from school. In winter it was nearly dark by the time we wound our way up to the cottage, the road narrow and steep with no pavement. I'd bring up the rear, carrying a torch and using a big white plastic carrier bag as a reflector, so we'd be seen at a distance.

'That hubby of yours should see he picks you up,' Mr Prosser said one evening when we'd all bundled in. 'It's not safe for you, walking in the dark on this hill. In fact it's bloody dangerous.'

'Danny always picks us up when he can,' I said, defending him as usual. Why, for heavens sake? 'He does have late lectures....'

Mr Prosser remained unimpressed. Strange, though I knew then, and had always known, I suppose, that our life with Danny left a lot to be desired, I still chose to live in this myth of my own making. Precariously constructed it might be, but I'd be hanging on to it for a good while yet. It was necessary.

The wet trees on the hill blurred past as we rattled up in the van, the inside of it steamy with the smell of damp tarpaulins.

'What's he actually studying at the college, then?' Thick eyebrows rose sceptically.

'International Politics and Strategic Studies,' I said, hoping to be warmed by the bewilderment and awe that proudly ringing title evoked. But not with Mr. Prosser.

'Really?' he said.

I'd heard the terrible rows, of course. Who could miss them? The shouting, especially at night. Those sons of his, and I never did work out whether there were three of them or just the two, they looked so alike, tall, spindly, with that thin red hair and those pale eyes, back from The Drover, I suppose, having had a skinful, and Mr Prosser, who never touched a drop, reading the riot act. I'd never seen Mrs Prosser, or so I thought. And it was only months after meeting the apple thief in the orchard that I realised who she was.

It was a long thin strip of an orchard, hugging the steep gradient, looking out on the wildness of sky without end, the valley below us, the foel opposite, with, in certain splashes of light, the old shapes of the Bronze Age ramparts, gilded clear, a darker green against bleached grass the colour of sand. She worked very softly. Without sound. Almost without movement. There was a liquid air in the orchard. Scented and thick with a low hum in it, not of insects, but of time, I think, swimming in lemony honey, catching all the past harvests of damsons and pears and tickling grass, russet butterflies like specks of autumn. But it was the apples she wanted. There was a crate by her feet, not a cardboard box, but a good strong wooden crate. She filled it slowly, deliberately, taking each apple and searching it first for blemishes. I wasn't angry. There was something quite honest and right about what I saw. We were the strangers here. This was her place.

I coughed gently, stood by the gate. Then again, louder. This time she looked up. There was a more obvious heaviness about her now. An exhaustion you could almost touch. And I think, but I'm not sure, I caught in my mind's eye the face of that prophet, his beard with its streaks of dull grey gunmetal, the eyes, so unlike hers, so dark. Opaque. But how could that be when I didn't know who she was? She'd appeared out of nowhere. She could have been anyone.

And to say that I caught my breath at her beauty sounds ridiculous. And anyway she wasn't beautiful. What was it then? She was tallish, quite thick set. There was something old-fashioned.... Her hair was folded in a loose French pleat, stray gold threads lay askew and damp on her neck. Like tendrils. Her arms were bare and her hands were a workman's. That's how I saw them. Spatualate fingers. Dirt thick under the nails. They were strong, capable hands. And her eyes, well, they were the palest blue, light with gold flecks in them. I didn't want to stare.

I tried to tell Danny about her that evening. There were no words to explain the impression she'd made. I could say what I'd seen. I could describe her. Everything. The dress she was wearing, thin cotton stained colourless with sweat under the arms, the scratched pale legs and the canvas summer shoes, split down the side. I could tell him all that but I couldn't get what I meant across to him.

'Are you sure she wasn't drunk?'

'Quite sure.'

'Are you sure you weren't?'

I just looked at him.

'They make some pretty wild scrumpy round here, you know,' he was smiling that annoying smile of his, 'but I've never heard of the smell of apples going to someone's head before.'

'Don't be stupid, Danny.'

'Is she going to make a habit of stealing our apples?'

'She said she'd been given permission by Mr Wynne. Anyway, there's far more of them than we could ever use.'

'Who is she anyway?'

'I don't know.'

And I didn't till the following May, late May that is. It had been very hot. Stifling. But a thin breeze had blown up from somewhere. I forget sometimes that as the crow flies we're only two or three miles from the sea. Anyway there we were, sat outside the cottage. All of us. And quiet with it, even the boys, who for once weren't squabbling. A kind of late evening siesta. It was just too hot to go back inside. Being built of stone and half clutched into the bank behind us the house retains heat. The bedrooms are little ovens.

It was Lisa spotted her. There's a steep drop in front of the cottage, just below the bird table Danny rigged up when we moved in.

'Look,' she said pointing down the tilting field. It was in shadow, all the light of the summer sky pouring like syrup on the foel in front of us. There was a woman walking with a dog down there, moving in and out of the shade, one moment in semi-darkness, the next in brilliant slanting sun, in and out of the alders and the fractured old willows that follow the river.

Right now it's almost a trickle. That comforting background murmur's gone. And there's been something unnatural about this dryness, this heat. A kind of extremity we're just not used to at all.

'It's that Mrs Prosser. Look, mum. I've never seen her outside before. What's she doing down there?'

'Who?' I said, 'Where? Danny, look. It's our apple thief. I'd know her anywhere. Mrs Prosser! Would you believe? How do you know it's her, Lisa?'

'I've seen her from the hay loft at Drws y Nen, when I go round to Bethan's. You can see right over their wall. I've seen her in the garden she's made there. It's all pebbles in patterns and shapes. Bethan says Mr Prosser doesn't let her out. She must have escaped.'

'What a load of rubbish,' said Danny. 'I've never heard such a load....'

He walked to the edge by the bird table and looked down. 'It's Prosser's dog all right,' he said laughing. And that was typical of Danny. As if people existed just so he could be amused by their strange ways. 'I'm glad it's managed to escape anyway. I hate to see an animal chained up like that.' He looked at me sideways. 'Your goddess of the orchard looks quite normal to me. And at least that dog's getting some exercise.'

'I didn't say anything about a goddess of the orchard,' I said.

'Course not,' said Danny.

That night I couldn't sleep. It just didn't seem to go dark at all. I lay there quietly for ages, listening to Danny's soft breathing, watching the light on the ceiling. Light? This wasn't moonlight. Great loops and bowls of light were swirling round the room, a sharp brightness catching each thread in the weft of the curtain. It was as if someone was swivelling a torch against our window. From outside. I had to have a look, slipping cautiously, slitheringly, out of bed. I didn't want Danny to wake, and, strangely, I wasn't in the least bit nervous. I just wanted to know. The foel was magical. Yes, and I'm quite sure there's some perfectly straightforward meteorological explanation. All this strange heat and stillness. A rare atmospheric phenomenon. Something like that. But I don't care. This silent summer lightning, whatever it was, neither bolts nor flashes, a tremulous glow, silvery, evanescent, coming and going as if playing an elaborate game of hide and seek with anyone lucky enough to watch it, enchanting the bare hillside.... I've never seen anything like it before. And I'll never forget it.

My feet were cool on the tiled floor in the kitchen. I grabbed my coat and turned the key, and I was out. Incredulous at first. The whole sky was filled with ethereal light. Standing there, knowing just what it must have been like to be one of those Bronze Age people in their hill fort on the foel across the valley. What it must have been like to worship the sun, the moon, the magic and awe of a night like this. I walked up to the gate that opens into the orchard. And it was then I heard the footsteps. I admit it — I was scared. I leaned back in to the shadows, holding my breath. They were hurried, urgent steps and they passed. Breathe again. Now I was creeping softly on damp grass to the top gate so I could see. If it hadn't been for the dog I wouldn't have been sure. But it was her all right. Mrs Prosser. And this time it looked as if she was escaping for good, with a suitcase in her hand and a swift sense of purpose.

The rain's stopped now. It's just the wind I can hear, no more of that slippery pull against the window. And there's no real darkness in a town, is there? They don't know what the real blackness of night is. Always there's that orange glow, the hum of hundreds and thousands of people....

Scream, Scream

It is quiet on the ward. There are only three bed patients. Nurse Sandra looks at her watch. It is so still. There is a faint hum of a mechanical mower on lawns far away, that is all. No birds are singing. Mrs Jessop is snoring quietly. She's had a bad night. It is on the report.

Linda is about to make her move. Nurse Sandra senses it. She smooths her apron, flicks through a magazine with studied carelessness watching sideways through her hair as Linda shifts her slow carcase off the bed. Even now as those bare arms emerge Nurse Sandra has to steel herself. She looks up, clenched. Sioned, the anorexic girl in the top bed is semaphoring wildly. Linda begins.

'Is my heart still beating?'

'Yes, Linda.'

Nurse Sandra tries to smile. How well she knows this never ending litany.

'Are you sure?'

'Yes.'

'Can you hear it?'

'Not from here I can't, no.'

'Come and listen.'

'Again, Linda?'

'Yes, I think it's stopped.'

'No luv, silly. Course it hasn't stopped. You wouldn't be sitting up talking to me if it had stopped, would you?'

'No.'

'There you are then.'

Now the familiar pause.

'Is my baby dead?'

This was the bit she dreaded. Day after day, hour after hour, the same question. And still she dreaded it.

'It's a long time ago now, Linda.'

'How long?'

'Two years.'

'I killed my baby didn't I?'

'No, you didn't kill your baby. You know you didn't.'

'Heroin killed my baby.'

'Yes.'

'Not me.'

'No.'

'But I did really. I know I did.'

Nurse Sandra gulps. Linda never wants platitudes. Sometimes she'll accept them. Mostly she won't.

Nurse Sandra still finds she winces inside at the sight of those arms; the half-healed scars she'd cleaned of pus months before are still lurid among the tattoos, the roses, crowns and mermaids, the names JIMMY and MOTHER, the waste, the pointlessness. Linda is dying. Her liver, which is all of twenty-three years old, is ready to pack up on her. She has respiratory problems. Her legs are hideously ulcerated. She has come here to die because there is nowhere else for her to go.

'Have you got a fag?'

'I don't smoke, Linda.'

'Mrs Jessop smokes.'

'Mrs Jessop is asleep.'

'When she wakes up?'

'You can ask her when she wakes up.'

'Will she give me a fag?'

'She usually does, doesn't she?'

'She usually does.'

A giggle. The ghost of a giggle.

'She always gives me a fag to make me go away.'

Linda is not averse to exploiting the unnerving effect she has on people, and Mrs Jessop is easily unnerved. So is Sioned. Linda changes tack. She knows the answer before she asks the question but she wants a reaction. She wants to see those dark eyes close, that pale skull shake its negative.

'You don't smoke, do you Sioned?'

Sioned is pretending not to be here. She does it well. She is now so thin she hardly makes a ripple under the blankets. She is disappearing. Tonic insulin seems not to have had the desired effect. She is seventeen, always tiny, admittedly, but now she weighs just four stone.

Mrs Jessop sputters into consciousness. Stretches, yawns, sits bolt upright.

'Oh.'

'Good morning Mrs Jessop. For this relief much thanks.'

Nurse Sandra walks up to the bed.

'How are we this morning?'

Mrs Jessop can't remember how she is. Bleary still from night sedation, she blinks, owl like, registers Linda's looming presence and makes an instinctive move for her handbag, proffering the packet.

Linda beams.

'Ta, Mrs Jessop. You're alright, you are. You'll be going home soon.'

She slouches off to the top of the ward again.

'If you're going to smoke you can go to the sitting room, Linda.'

'Aw, just this once, Sandra.'

'Sitting room.'

'Can I go in the wheelchair, then?'

'You know I can't push you. I can't leave the ward.'

'There's only Mrs Jessop and Sioned, Sandra. Nothing's going to happen while you push me that little way. It's not far.'

'If you want to smoke you go to the sitting room and if you want to go to the sitting room you have to walk.'

'You're a tight bitch, Sandra.'

'Yeah, I'm a real hard case.'

'Can I have a light, Mrs Jessop?'

'Not on the ward, Linda.'

'I wasn't talking to you. I was talking to Mrs Jessop.'

There is an edge in Linda's voice but she no longer has the energy to put that edge into action. Nurse Sandra gives her a look.

Now it's a battle of wills and Sandra will win because she has the will to win and Linda has not. The girl's efforts have already exhausted her. She wants her cigarette but she does not want to haul herself down the corridor to smoke it. In the end the cigarette wins. It always does. She starts to move down the ward again, painfully slowly for Sandra's benefit, holding on to the beds.

'Can I borrow your lighter, Mrs Jessop?'

'Get a light from someone down there.'

'There won't be anyone down there. They've gone to OT.'

'Get a light from Sister Annie, then.'

'Where?'

'In the office.'

'Is that where she is?'

'Yes.'

'Are you sure? Is she on her own?'

'It's not time for the doctors to make their round yet, Linda, if that's what you're worried about.'

'Is Dr Patel on today?'

'I don't know.'

'She's on holiday,' says Mrs Jessop.

'Is she? How do you know?'

'She told me.'

Linda looks sulky. She likes to think she has a special relationship with Dr Patel, that she is her confidante. To compensate for not having received this piece of information she makes an extravagant balletic swoop towards Mrs Jessop, hands moulded in parodic impression of an Indian dancer's.

'She's promised me one of her old saris, Dr Patel has. She said I could have one. She likes me.'

'You've been pestering her again, haven't you?' Nurse Sandra cuts in, wishing Linda would really get off the ward and go for her smoke. Linda glowers.

'I like Dr Patel. She's alright.'

In a moment of rare humour Mrs Jessop chuckles to herself. 'She'll be going home soon.'

Nurse Sandra smiles. 'She's got a long way to go.'

Just then the scream.

A vehicle must have drawn up, but they didn't hear it. The front doors have opened and the scream has come in has forced itself in, breaking through their innocuous recitative. This is the aria, a full blooded aria.

They hear the office door click shut. But they couldn't have heard it above the scream. They must have just sensed it. They are, after all, alive to the relevance of all the building's distinctive vibrations. Nurse Sandra finds herself standing at attention. It's that kind of scream. Joyce, the cleaner, emerges from the toilets, mop akimbo.

'Christ,' she says, 'What's this?'

This is Mrs Jenkins. This is Mrs Jenkins' scream. The scream is on a stretcher. Sister Annie is standing by, keys jingling, along with two ambulancemen and a small fair nurse who looks no more than a child.

'Hello Mrs Jenkins,' says Sister Annie. They seem to have met. Curtains are whisked round a bed. The scream seems to fill the world. It changes pitch, it warbles, it fluctuates, it recedes, but it never stops. Sister Annie knows this scream, consequently it holds fewer fears for her. Mrs Jessop is sat bolt upright again, clutching her capacious handbag. Linda hovers, cigarette forgotten. Even Sioned is suddenly transformed into an unusually animated skeleton. She grabs her housecoat from the bed-rail behind her and the emaciated arms disappear into an incongruous protective blur of pink frills. Her mouth falls agape. More arrivals. Dr Merton (nobody likes Dr Merton) and Dr Patel, who is not on holiday after all. They disappear behind the curtain. Blending into the scream are the soft cooing sounds of Sister Annie, Dr Patel's staccato, the young nurse's uncertain burble and Dr Merton's stentorian boom. It is a virtuoso performance. Now the ambulancemen retreat. Now Dr Merton and the young nurse retreat. Only Sister Annie and Dr Patel remain behind the curtain, as the scream breaks the sound barrier and Sioned starts to cry. Nurse Sandra rushes up the ward, reassuring the pink mist until it sinks again beneath the candle-wick. Joyce the Cleaner, ever reliable appears with the tea trolley, basking in virtue, since This Is Not Really Her Job, but we're so short staffed this morning, what with Nurse Margaret on ECT and

Nurse Meira called to take that awful Mrs Prendergast for another EEG last minute. Joyce pours tea copiously, wearing her Very Dependable Face. And still the scream, the scream. Perhaps the ambulancemen have left the doors open, though there seemed to be no wind. Now there's a Force Nine Gale. The curtains around the vexed bed billow, the curtains at the windows float in a strange leeward drift, the lampshades swing. Very Dependable Joyce proffers tea to all, with the exception of Mrs Jenkins who can't be expected to scream and drink tea at the same time.

It's as if the scream slowly inhabits them all, slowly expresses them all. It's as if the terror slowly seeps out of it, while another nameless quality enters. What does it consist of, this blend of dark voices beyond Mrs Jenkins' own, far beyond, ungovernable, timeless voices without meaning or order, but shot through with a rhythm they recognise, a substance they have felt themselves, all of them, the Hell's Angel and the nursing sister, the anorexic girl who won't grow up and the doctor who has torn up her roots and crossed the world to do just that, the cleaner who is pompous and kind and commonsensical and the wife of the managing director who is childless and bereft, a loss for which no amount of jewels and furs and foreign holidays can compensate. Perhaps most of all it is Nurse Sandra's scream, since she's been walking on the edge for weeks now, though no one would ever know. She swims with the scream as it ripples and bellows, rises and falls. It is a medley of voices, the cry of aftermath, of battle and birth, of sap and sinew. Mrs Jenkins cannot know that her scream is a beneficence, that she takes from all of them their fears, relaying them back, transformed, intensified and finally transcended, that the ward's bland pastels fuse into whirling primary shades, a vortex of richness, of wildness, of courage. It takes courage, this truth, this scream.

Dr Patel and Sister Annie have decided on their course of action. The curtains are whisked back from the bed. Propped up against pillows lies a wizened face, but you can't really tell it's a wizened face at the moment because all you can see at the moment is the mouth. It is so wide open it seems to have taken over, engulfing all. Sioned, huddled under the covers, still cushions her ears with her hands. Nurse Sandra has turned quite white. Linda stands by the bed, unlit cigarette in hand. Mrs Jessop makes strange popping noises like a frog.

Mrs Jenkins comes from a farm, a farm in the middle of nowhere. A farm so old it's like a great fungus, an excrescence of the land, breeding barns and byres full of rusting threshing machines and ancient harrows and flails. Enough to fill a museum with fascinating glimpses of our agricultural past. But this isn't the past. It's the present. Little has changed at Sgubor Fawr since Owain Glyndwr rode by, swelling his army with the sons of the farm, only one of whom returned, an ancestor of Mrs Jenkins' lawful wedded spouse. She was a Jenkins too, before her marriage, since there were only Jenkinses to be found for miles around. But this is the end of the line. The very end. This is the scream of the last of the Jenkinses of Sgubor Fawr, this is.

It's unforgettable.

There's an hour and ten minutes to go till the others come back from OT. Dr Patel and Sister Annie will let her scream till then. She's screamed solid since half-past-seven last night, according to Mr Jenkins who is usually reliable in these matters. She's screamed in the ambulance for thirty-seven miles by green lane and new road. (Mrs Jenkins never leaves Sgubor Fawr except to come here. It is rumoured she went to Shrewsbury in Coronation Year, but that tale might well be apocryphal.) Who knows, by dinner time it might be all over. She might have done with screaming. Until the next time.

Very Dependable Joyce is handing out a second cup of tea to those who want. All drink. Even Sioned, submerged in her pink haze,drinks but it's the eating she won't do, isn't it? She's in such a state of shock she almost accepts a Nice biscuit from Joyce's Own Personal Packet. But then she remembers she's anorexic and politely refuses. The scream keeps going, keeps flowing. Dr Merton makes a grim appearance at the ward door, shrugs and disappears. Nurse Sandra stands by. Sister Annie and Dr Patel sit and wait and listen. Is that a diminuendo? Surely...yes...no. The scream has risen again but it's definitely less screamy, this scream. It's on the wane. It wobbles, it fades, it flickers, it stops. It finally stops.

Mrs Jenkins does not look sheepish. She is not in the least embarrassed. She has the most ferret-like face you've ever seen. A swarthy ferret with black pebble eyes. In her high bird-like voice she asks Joyce if she can go home now. Very Dependable Joyce explains that as she is the Cleaner it's not really up to her to say. But tea she does have to offer.

'It'll be a bit stewed by now. I'll make you fresh if you like.'

'No lovey,' says Mrs Jenkins who is invariably easy to please. 'I'm sure it will taste fine. I like my tea strong.'

I bet you do, thinks Nurse Sandra.

It's still on the ward. Now there's not even the faint hum of a mechanical mower. It's an extraordinary stillness. Not a silence as such, more a resonant absence. How wonderful it is to hear the scream has gone. Never has any silence felt this peaceful, more like velvet, more gentle, more deep. Goodness is singing in the ward. Without making a sound.

Dr Patel winks conspiratorially at Sister Annie. Dr Merton was wrong, wasn't he? He wanted to give her morphine. They said leave her alone.

And they did.

And it worked.

It has happened before, of course. Every three years since 1953, the year of the Coronation, the year Mrs Jenkins went to Shrewsbury. If she did.

She will be going home in a day or two. She'll be chatting away to those two nice ambulancemen who brought her in this morning, sirens blaring. Well, it's all in a day's work.

Linda is now en route to the sitting room. Sioned lies quietly, thinking. Mrs Jessop is rooting anxiously in her handbag. Strange, she seems to have mislaid her lighter. The electrician comes in to change the dud bulb above Mrs Jenkins' bed.

At Sgubor Fawr the sun has filtered briefly through the trees. Mr Jenkins is feeding the hens.

Helping the Police With Their Enquiries

Who's the ponce in the hat?' I said, and you hissed through your teeth, 'Why do you have to pretend to be such a philistine? You're such a prat, Reg. Really.'

I can't believe that was our last conversation. And yet, here I am, pinching myself to prove I'm not dreaming, as the police set about digging up the garden. They're very systematic. They've already torn the house apart, even down to lifting the floorboards and removing the new pine panelling in the extension.

'Coffee, Dad?' That's Stella. She's supposed to be in Brussels with the school choir. Instead she's opted to stay with me in a valiant attempt to keep me sane.

'I keep wanting to tell you to stop worrying, but it sounds so stupid.' She looks so like you, Jane, when she creases her face like that. 'How can you *not* worry, for Christ's sake?'

I squeeze her hand, choke back the noises I want to make. I want to scream. Scream out at the world. I have NOT, repeat NOT killed my wife. Half hiding behind the curtain I look down the road. It seems quiet enough. The gentlemen of the press have given up on me even if the police haven't. From their point of view it looks bad. It has to. Everyone knows spouses are first in line as suspects.

Had we quarrelled? I gave them our last words. Verbatim. But the tone doesn't come through. The affection in it. It was a sort of game. You were the arty one, the cultured one, but even in that last rejoinder of yours, you weren't fooled. Why must you pretend to be such a philistine, that's what you said. And if I was a prat it was because I pretended. A kind of pseud philistine. I suppose it must've been bloody annoying. A habit.

But men don't kill their wives because they call them prats. Anyway, we've been talking like that for years. That didn't stop us caring about each other. In our weird way. Lots of marriages I can think of are a lot more weird than ours. What's the best thing can happen now? Am I willing them to find a body? What a thing to wish for! And yet as the days go by I can't believe you're still alive. You'd never put me through this willingly. Anything's better than this, though, surely.... There's nothing worse than this not knowing at all.

Oh yes there is.... Stella brings me the coffee I didn't ask for. It's just something to do.

* * * * *

Looking back I can't help feeling there was something strange about the place. Wise after the event I suppose. There was this sense, of what, timelessness I think. As if we'd stepped right out of the twentieth century. As if the rest of the world had just stopped.

We had to park the car at the top and walk down. It had been raining. As we drove across the moors there was this thick mist but it lifted as we neared the coast. Walking down the steep gradient you could smell the sea. All the roofs were shiny after rain, the twisting streets silvery with it. In the narrow gardens the earth, dry for weeks, seemed to be breathing. There was a kind of steamy effect. Humid, and all the colours were bright.

You grabbed my hand. 'This place is just perfect, Reg, I'm so glad we came.'

You'd expect a place like that to be commercialised. Totally. You know, little shops bulging with gimcrack souvenirs and sticks of rock, but it wasn't. You didn't find a shop that sold postcards till we got right down to the harbour. That was the first thing we did. Or you did. You bought a dozen of them, sent me to get some stamps, and started writing. 'If I get all these done now I can forget about them.'

'Right,' I said.

In the window of the post office there was a display of jet

jewellery. I wondered if you'd like something, thought I might buy you one of those brooches later. Not that you ever wear brooches, but still.... I noticed that the harbour was a proper harbour, with real fishing boats, none of those fancy landlubbers' yachts. A river of sorts, a trickle really, came down into the cove through a narrow cleft and on one side there were cliffs, heavily eroded, scattered with gulls, kittiwakes you said they were, and swathes of yellow-white droppings. I thought of those islands in the South Atlantic. Nothing but guano. And those birds just never shut up, not for a minute. Wail, wail, wail all day long, but I hadn't got to hate the sight and sound of them then. Not yet.

When I got back with the stamps you'd already written most of the cards. 'It's hard to think of something different to say,' you said. 'Why can't you write the same thing then?' I asked, reasonably enough I thought. 'Oh, I couldn't do that,' you said, indignant, 'Anyway people might compare.'

We decided we'd eat at a big white rambling pub on the other side of the cove, away from all those gulls. All that wailing and all that crap. We weren' t hungry though, so we thought we'd explore a bit first. That's when we came across the gallery. It overlooked the inner harbour, where all those small fishing boats were moored together in a tangle of lines, as if they were insects stuck in a web. It was a strange thing to think of, that. I distinctly remember shivering, and God knows it wasn't in the least bit cold.

Then I recognised that eager, even predatory look on your face. You'd seen the gallery. *Yves Marechal — contemporary watercolours*, the flamboyant sign announced, at which point I volunteered to post the cards and disappeared. What I could see through the window struck me as pretentious daubs, but then I pretend to be a philistine, don't I?

Afterwards I followed you quietly round the gallery. You didn't know I'd come back. I saw you take off your sunglasses and appraise each painting. Studied nonchalance. It made me want to laugh. God, I'm sorry. Hovering in the background was the aforementioned ponce, Yves Marechal himself, no doubt. He was wearing a white linen suit and yes, a hat, a panama. I decided his real name was something very ordinary. He'd become Yves Marechal in order to impress susceptible ladies like yourself. It was with deeply cynical and unkind thoughts such as these that I approached you, uttered the fatal words in a stage whisper, and received the surprisingly savage reply.

'*Why do you have to pretend to be such a philistine? You're such a prat, Reg. Really.*'

And are those the last words I'll ever hear you say?

Stella's voice stuns me back again. 'You haven't drunk your coffee, Dad,' she says, just as one of the policemen emerges from the garden.

'You said your wife was carrying a camera, Mr. Fane.'

'Yes,' I reply, nervously now, since everything I say seems to make them more suspicious.

'It appears to have been found.'

'Oh,' I say numbly. 'Where?'

He didn't answer my question. I didn't expect him to. 'If you'll accompany us to the police station you might be able to confirm that it is in fact your wife's camera.'

'Of course,' I say. I follow him like an automaton.

'I'll come with you,' Stella rushes after me, dragging her coat from the stand in the hall. 'That won't be necessary, Miss Fane. W.P.C. Mackintosh will remain here with you until your father returns.'

'Do you really have to talk like bloody robots all the time?' I grumble, but feebly. I was getting to the point I couldn't take any more of it. Days of it. And now this about the camera. Was it all coming to an end? If they'd found that, didn't it mean they were about to find you? I didn't know what anything meant anymore. Everything was still wide open. Anyway, it might not even be your camera.

It was. What's more, before getting me down there, they'd got the film in it developed and the prints blown up. They handed me them, one after another. Slowly. Watching my reaction. And what was my reaction? When you know every twitch of your face is being scrutinised it has the strangest effect. My facial muscles went numb. I looked at the photographs. I looked up at their impassive faces. The two of them, Cosnett, who always seemed to give me the benefit of the doubt, and the other gingery one with the pale lashes. The clichés are all true after all. Mr Soft and Mr Hard. But it's never quite how you figure it's going to be. Ginger's pretty innocuous, I think, for all his sneers, his little tricks of innuendo. Cosnett, the humane and affable Cosnett, he's lethal.

I'm supposed to say something. 'Whoever took these photographs must've been on the cliffs.' The words seemed to belong to someone else.

'Yes, Mr Fane. But that isn't the most remarkable thing about them is it?'

'No.'

'What do you think the fact that you're in every one of these photographs tells us?'

'Somebody knew me. Knew us, perhaps....'

'So you don't think your wife took these photographs?'

'No. I can't think why she would. I mean why would she get up on those cliffs and take photographs of me looking for her?'

'So you were looking for her? The photographs don't actually tell us that.'

'No. But I've already told you that. I thought she'd meet me at the pub. We'd already decided we'd eat there. I waited till after two and then I went looking for her.'

'But you originally left her at the gallery. After your quarrel.'

'It wasn't a quarrel.'

'She called you a prat.'

'Yes. Don't keep telling me what I've already told you. For God's sake, you're raking over the same old ground all the time. These photographs, I don't know what they mean....'

'Nor do we, Mr Fane....'

'...but they must mean something. And why did whoever it was who took them leave the camera behind? If it was deliberate....'

'But we don't know that it was. It's taken some finding. It wasn't in an obvious place. Perhaps there was a struggle. Perhaps, if we assume your wife was abducted, the camera was dropped in that struggle. Or thrown away.'

I still don't ask them where they found it. I want to know but I know they won't tell me. And I know I don't have to tell them anything either. But I'm helping the police with their enquiries, Jane. That's all. I've got nothing to hide. I want them to find you. Dead or alive, Jane. You've got to be found.

'You still insist your wife wasn't having an affair....'

'I don't insist anything. I don't know anything. I don't think she was having an affair. I would have known. I think I would've known. What's more, I think she would've told me.'

'Would she? How can you be sure?'

'Christ, I'm not sure. Our marriage had its ups and downs, but we said what we thought. We meant what we said. We didn't hide things.'

'So what's your theory? What do these photographs tell you?'

'I don't have a theory. All I know is I can't see why Jane would take them. And I've already told you *that*. They're almost all the same. Exactly. The same view, taken from exactly the same place. And they're all of me looking for her. It's like a sick joke.'

'A practical joke, perhaps?'

'No. She'd never bother with anything so childish.'

'So somebody else took them. O.K. And you immediately thought that meant the person who took them knew you. As a couple. Before. Is that likely?'

'I don't mean knew us. Had seen us together, that's all.... Then saw us apart. I don't know, but if Jane was abducted somebody could've taken the photographs later. He'd either,' I can't bear to say this, Jane, 'bundled her into a car, or something, and then come back and taken these photographs of me. And that is a sick joke. Or there were two people.'

'How d'you reckon that, Mr Fane?'

That was Ginger. He's like a weasel, Jane. Shifty and sharp. A gingery weasel. And Cosnett's got a strong face, the sort of man you'd like on your side. And he is on your side. He wants to find you, that's his whole intention. One way or another, he wants just that. But Ginger just wants to nail me. Wants me nailed whether I'm guilty or not. And Christ knows I'm not guilty. You know that Jane, wherever you are.

I look Ginger in the eye and I can't hide my loathing. 'If two people were involved one could have held on to Jane while the other took the photographs. But it doesn't make sense at all.'

'No,' says Ginger. 'It doesn't. Let me just tell you my theory, shall I? Not so much a theory, more a working hypothesis. Let's call it that for now. Like you, I think two people were involved. Difference is I think one of them was you, Fane. I think you killed your wife. How and where I'm not sure. Not yet. All we know for certain is that you were in that gallery, both of you, at approximately twenty to one. Witnesses can confirm that, and the proprietor noticed you leaving after just a couple of minutes. Just you.

'Your wife had been looking round before your arrival, and was there for some fifteen minutes after you'd left. You'd had some sort of quarrel. The proprietor confirms that too. Didn't hear what was said but registered some sort of major disagreement, or shall we say difference of opinion. He saw you leave in the direction of the harbour. Mrs Fane, he noticed, eventually left in the opposite direction. At approximately two o'clock the girl behind the bar at The Anchor confirms that you bought a pint of their best bitter and asked whether a lady, a blonde, wearing jeans and a green blouse, had been in. She replied in the negative. You took your drink outside, but first of all you told the barmaid your wife was supposed to be meeting you there, and hadn't arrived. It was already too late to order a meal in the restaurant, but bar snacks were apparently still available. You said you'd be sitting outside. You'd noticed there were two entrances to The Anchor, the one you'd used into the public bar, and another at the side of the building which led into the restaurant. You asked the barmaid to keep an eye open in case the lady in the green blouse etc. entered from that direction but she told you that once the last few remaining customers had finished their meal, that door would be locked until the evening. There was no way, with you sitting right outside the one door, that you could miss your wife. The barmaid remembers you struck her as being particularly nervous and uneasy....'

'I was,' I said. 'Of course I was. I'd already been looking for Jane for almost an hour by then.'

'I don't think so, Mr Fane. An hour is a long time. Quite long enough for you to have killed you wife and disposed of the body....'

40

'But this is ridiculous!' I look at Cosnett. Why does he let him go on? They're just winding me up. They must be. Both of them. 'I'm trying to help you. I've told you everything. I've co-operated with you in every way. You can't hold me here. You haven't charged me.'

'That's quite right, Mr Fane.' It's Cosnett this time. His face is calm, his tone entirely reasonable. He's not like that runt. That Ginger. 'We haven't charged you. We need to know who took the photographs. We need to know who your accomplice was.'

'This is crazy. Why are you doing this? Those photographs prove I didn't kill her.'

'Do they? I don't think so. We have several witnesses who vouch for the fact that you spent the rest of the afternoon looking for your wife. You asked several people if they'd seen her. Of course you did. You wanted it all to fit. But we know that not one of those photographs of you, the supposedly distraught husband, was taken during that crucial hour between one and two.'

I sit there, trying to take it in. Jane this can't be true. It can't be. I think of Stella at home with that W.P.C. Mackintosh. They'll be putting the pressure on her, poor kid. What will she say?

'Wouldn't it be better if you told us the truth, Mr Fane? We know there was an accomplice. There has to be. And just take another look at these photographs. Look at the shadows. You can see for yourself. If they'd been taken between one and two when the sun was still pretty well at its height, there would have been no shadows. All these photographs have been taken between three o'clock and five, possibly even later. We know something else, Mr Fane. The ticket attendant at the car park remembers your car arriving. He's quite adamant there were three people in it. He noticed it when you drove in because he couldn't help but see that the passenger in the back was extremely distressed. Crying, he said. You never said there was a third person with you, Mr Fane. Or that the quarrel with your wife, far from starting that afternoon in the gallery, was pretty much an on-going thing. It's not difficult to imagine a fifteen year old girl trying to salvage something from the wreckage by covering up for her father. There was nothing she could do to bring her mother back. Did she have to lose her father too?'

'I want to see a solicitor.'

'Yes, Mr Fane. I think you probably should. Incidentally, it was reported that a teenage girl had been seen on the cliffs on the afternoon of your wife's disappearance, but we didn't see the relevance of that until we found the camera. You sent her up there, didn't you? To take those photographs. You made it far too complicated. Panic, was it? Makes people do the strangest things. We know Stella didn't actually see you kill her mother. It might have been different if she had, but she left you in the car park, didn't she? Ran off, upset, we're told, towards the coastguard station on the West Brows, and only turned up again about three o'clock, looking for you both around the harbour. Was it out of love she colluded with you, Mr Fane? Fear, perhaps? Or was it one of those interesting conditions in between?'

I don't look up at Cosnett's face, Jane. Stella was always so much like you, wasn't she? Like mother, like daughter, eh? Pity I didn't finish her off too. You were quite right about me. A prat of the first order. And that poor, pretty little bitch.... I just couldn't bring myself to do it.

Future Perfect

No. Not there. More to the right.'
'Here?'
'Yes. Now try.'
I breathe in deeply.
'Well?'
'All I can smell is a mixture of incense and that air freshener stuff you've been squirting around.'
'M'mm. You should've smelt it this morning. Terrible it was. I've phoned the council. I think it's a disgrace.'
I bite my tongue. I don't ask the obvious question. Shouldn't a clairvoyant know in advance when to leave well alone? I mean, if there's going to be a problem with the drains wouldn't there be a prior wobble on the astral plane or somewhere?
'You been to see me before?'
'No?'
'Sure?'
'Quite sure'
'Not when I had the booth on the prom, outside the Majestic?'
'No.'
'M'mm. Could've sworn I'd seen you before.'
'Perhaps you have. I've lived here, well, round about, for years.'
'Not on holiday then?'
'No.'
'Working?'
Now this Gipsy Hayes is persistent. I'll give her that. I don't know what her palmistry's like but she's got a good line in interrogation. And her Apache squaw look helps. That expression. Deep. Intense. Mysterious.
Suddenly she laughs, relaxes.
'I know you, now.'

'Really?'

'Yes. I never forget a face, lady. Can't afford to, not in this line of business.'

'Suppose not. That makes sense.' I smile. 'But I assure you I've never come here before.'

'I know that. And I know where I've seen you. In the paper.'

What do I say? I don't say anything. I don't have to.

'It's not usually you in the paper, is it lady? I mean, you don't supply the news. You write it. Right?'

I give in. She's astute, this one. And I'm not *that* hard-boiled.

'Well, Gipsy Hayes. I've got to hand it to you. You've blown my cover. I cannot tell a lie, which is a lie, but what the hell? If I'm a journalist so what? Needn't make any difference, need it?'

'You going to do a write up on me?'

'Not just you.'

'Madame Welinski?'

'The lot. I'm doing the coast. All the clairvoyants, palmists, crystal ball readers. You name it. A kind of *Which* guide to Fortune Tellers. Rest assured I'll be scrupulously fair. But tell me something. My picture's only been in the paper once and that was last year, just before Christmas. And I've had my hair cut short since then.'

'Like I said, elephants and Gipsy Hayes never forget. Won an award, didn't you?'

'Yes. Nothing to get excited about. Very local.'

'Don't put yourself down, lady. The world will always do that for you. Be proud of what you can do. I am.'

'You're good, are you?'

'Find out.'

'I intend to.'

'So what did you think of Madame Welinski?'

I tap my nose. 'Sorry. Confidential. You'll have to wait and see.'

'You weren't impressed.'

'Wasn't I?'

'That woman's not well. Gallstones. Should see a doctor. She won't, of course.'

'Know her then, do you? Have professional exchanges?'

'You could say that.' She laughs again, richly. It's a confident, comfortable laugh. This woman certainly has something. Aplomb. Panache. I think I like her. But it's weird being scrutinised, being on the other side of the fence for a change, and Gipsy Hayes is certainly scrutinising me. Eyes like a laser.

'Right,' she says, straightens her skirt. Businesslike. No nonsense.

'Gipsy Hayes is always better for a cup of tea. Care to join me?'

'O.K. Why not? You can't bribe me with a cup of tea, though.'

'Bribe you?' She positively cackles. 'I don't need to do that lady.'

She disappears behind the bead curtain. The joss stick twitches. A little soft ash falls. Now she's back with a flask and two polka dot mugs.

'Could boil a kettle here, mind you, but I don't trust the water.'

'Connected to the drains, is it?'

'Tastes like it. Nothing would surprise me about this place. And if you want to know why I rented it I'll tell you. When they decided to give the Majestic a face lift my booth didn't fit in with their new image, did it? Had to sling my hook. At short notice. Landed here. I've got my eye on a good pitch for next season.'

'You're a bit tucked away here.'

'Yes. And it's not cheap. I'm not going to put up with the stink on top of the inconvenience. They'll have to do something.'

'Turn the Drainage Department into black beetles if they don't?'

'Cheeky, cheeky. You ready?'

'Yes.'

'Right.'

'How much do you charge?'

'Depends.'

'How much do you mean to charge me?'

'Ten pounds.'

'Twice as much as Madame Welinski.'

'I'm twice as good as Madame Welinksi. And you pay in advance.'

I open my purse , hand her two five pound notes.

'Both hands, please.'

'Both?'

'Yes.'

I place both hands palm side up on the table. The cloth is green chenille.

'M'mm. You've got two reasons for seeing me.'

I keep my mouth shut. I don't intend to give her any leads. It's my turn to study her face. Humorous. Sceptical. Leathery skin. Does she drink? Is it the Romany blood? She'd claim it was. She looks different now. She's concentrating. The Apache squaw look's been switched on again. It's a good act, I'll give her that. And she does emanate a certain power. Poise. Presence. It's hard to say just what it is. She's at ease with herself. Well I suppose she's an experienced trickster. There's no malice in it. If people are daft enough to part with their money for her to say the first thing that comes into her head that's their look out. She supplies a need. Fair enough. It's all pretty harmless. Now she jolts me back. Fixes me with those eagle eyes.

'You think you're above all this. You're the type who'd never go to see a palmist except to prove it's all a load of rubbish. I've met plenty like you. But this write up thing's an excuse. Convenient. That way you can hide the real reason for coming here. Even from yourself.'

I say nothing. I'm finding it difficult to sit still.

'You've got yourself into a mess lady. Don't know what to do. Don't know where to turn. You've got a child and that shiny ring don't fool me. You're in love with a man who doesn't want you.'

I try not to squirm. This plain gold band, third finger left hand certainly put Madame Welinksi off the scent. Mind you, I felt from the start that this one was in a different league. Still....

'You're kidding yourself lady. This man, this father of your child, he married?'

If that was a question I'm not going to answer it.

'You don't have to tell me anything. You're an open book. You're still hoping, aren't you? Still waiting. You're a fool to yourself. You'll never get him. He's got a wife. Three kids. He's older than you. Father figure? Grow up, lady. You're backing a loser. He'll wring you dry. And I don't mean money.'

I'm starting to twitch. I make an effort to keep my hands firmly on the table. But now she's lifted my hands, holds them loosely on her own. They're hot, they're cold. I feel....

'I'm getting something. Not his name. An initial. Definitely. It's a K. He's across the water. Travels a lot. Keeps coming back. Likes the kid. She's three, four, a pretty child, fair haired like him. Your mother looks after her while you're working, right? She keeps telling you, doesn't she? Forget him. Look for someone else. Right?'

I say nothing. To my annoyance my hands start to shake. Hers are rocklike.

'Keith. That's his name. I've got it. He's coming back this weekend. Flying. He's flying now. No. He's at an airport. Been delayed. You want to tell him you don't want to know. But you can't. You're torn in two lady. Heart and head. Heart says yes. Head tells you no. Head tells you finish. Heart tells you keep waiting. Keep hoping. It's all on his terms lady. But I'll tell you this. You're not the only one. I mean, apart from his wife. He's blackhearted, lady.'

'No.'

'No?'

I pull my hands away.

'No. He isn't like that.'

'Don't want to hear the truth? You don't have to hear it. You can walk out that door the way you came.'

I rub my hands. This ridiculous ring slips on my finger. I hear children outside. I hear traffic. Music. I want to get out.

'Heard enough lady?'

The Apache squaw stares at me. Unsmiling. Fierce. She frightens me.

'I...I think I've heard enough.'

'There's more.'

'I don't think I want more.'

'No? You're sure? You don't get a discount. But if you've heard enough, had enough....'

'No. Go on. I might as well.'

'In for a penny lady? Both hands please.'

This time she places her hands on mine. Such bony hands, light, dry, buzzing. Buzzing?

'Them who goes over the devil's back has got to crawl under his belly.'

'What?'

'Say it again? Them who goes over the devil's back has got to crawl under his belly.'

'Sorry. I don't...'

'Don't understand?'

'A wind lifts the bead curtain. A little, dry, insinuating wind. The joss stick shifts. A fall of ash. A lot this time. A soft grey avalanche of ash in the saucer.

'I don't understand either lady.'

She drops my hands. I feel her draw back. Pull away. Fade.

'Are you feeling ill?'

'No. I'm alright.'

I look at her. Gipsy Hayes couldn't turn pale if she tried. But her face....

'You got something of his? A letter, maybe?'

'I dig in my handbag. I hand her the thin blue airmail envelope. She takes it. Holds it.

'You want to hear this lady?'

I nod. There's no trickery here. Not now. Not even if there was before. This is real.

'There won't be no more letters lady. You ready? You prepared for this?' She rakes her long hands through her hair. Her voice grates. She is suddenly old.

'This has never happened before for me. Not like this. Never the moment of...'

'I know what it is.'

'Yes. I think you do. I'm sorry lady. Something like a bomb, I think. An explosion. He didn't feel a thing.'

'No,' I say softly. 'Not really. He never did. He never felt a thing.'

48

Seeds

Laurie moved along the wall carrying a bowl and a scissors. She was snipping off the poppy heads. Under each crown there were tiny apertures and as Laurie swiftly placed each poppy head in the bowl tiny dark seeds emerged, just a few each time. They littered the bowl's base, visible under the piled heads which now, in the shadow of the wall were the colour of savoury pastry. They were mysterious these seeds. Fine and rich like seed pearls. Later Laurie would shake them all loose, let them lie smooth and shining in her hand. She would let them slip through her fingers with a kind of relish and gather them together in a tin, the same tin she always used. It was a relic of childhood, an old toffee tin, the picture almost worn off now, showing remnants of kittens in remnants of a plaited straw basket.

Never had the poppies been this tall, this handsome. They'd looked artificial. Unreal somehow. Now they were over and summer was good as over too. The way the swallows kept playing their practice games, grouping and regrouping on the wires told everyone they were ready for off.

The poppy heads were dry and brittle, of a bleached papery colour. They were tough and the stalks were tough and as the wind rattled among them Laurie felt they might well be talking among themselves. That was a fanciful notion. Childish. She found these notions haunting her increasingly lately and it was with greater difficulty each time that she pushed them down. But push them down she did. She was afraid of them.

Laurie was restless. She knew why she was restless and that made it worse. She pushed the thought that made her restless down. But it was not a thought. It was a feeling and it kept bobbing back up. The feeling was one of anticipation. Her skin felt tingly and loose and her legs felt heavy. She moved along the wall as if she'd been drinking, wobbly, vague, not quite sure of where she was putting her feet. It was not an unpleasant feeling but it was a feeling she did not want. It made her feel she was not in control of herself.

She tried to concentrate on the poppy heads, the movements of her hands among the leathery stalks and the faded strips of leaves. She found herself counting the white stones that edged the border between the wall and the track. In winter this track would ooze mud alongside cloud-patched puddles but now it was deeply rutted, baked hard by the sun and dusty from the wheels of her neighbours' cars.

Laurie's was the last house in the row and the track was shared, a right of way for all of them. They all had to pass the poppies and they all complimented her on them. This year their compliments had reached lavish heights. Though she said it herself, that shouldn't, Laurie had to concede they'd been magnificent. Each year there seemed to be more colours, more variations. Subtle silk pink through to a deep flame shade, all with thick sooty centres. Laurie's poppies were famous.

She told herself she'd go inside now, make herself a cup of tea and write her letter to Brian and Shelley and the girls in Germany. That was a safe thing to do. It was a ritual. She often found it difficult to find things to say and wondered why she bothered. Brian's letters were as rare as snow in June and Shelley only wrote at Christmas but that was not the point. Even if Brian no longer made the effort to read her letters she would still make the effort to write. Big sister writes to little brother. Sometimes in bleak moments she came to the conclusion that she only wrote to prove she was still alive. In mischievous moments, and these were rare, she thought she'd actually write that down, say it out straight:

Dear Brian and Shelley,
    I'm writing this to prove I'm still alive,
       love,
          Laurie,

just to see what happened. But she'd better not. Brian would get worried and think she was cracking up, the way she did after her father died. He'd phone Mrs. Kubicz next door and there'd be hell to pay.

The seeds were in the tin and the tin was on the window sill in the sun. They'd stay there for a few weeks drying out nicely. Before the worst of the frosts she would turn the border over and plant the seeds as she always did. She'd plant them deep and next summer they'd make again an invaluable topic of conversation. My life is so predictable thought Laurie. It's just more of the same.

She drank her tea and flicked through the paper. In two hours time she'd be busy in the kitchens at *The Saracen's*. That was good. That was work. And there were other people. It got so hot in those kitchens the fire alarm went off sometimes and they had to open the fire doors. This made Laurie laugh anarchically, defrosting prawns under the hot tap or building an elaborate arrangement of lemon meringue and peach sorbet to the accompaniment of Gary doing his artistically obscene cucumber dance wearing only boxer shorts and a plastic apron. But the season was over now. Gary was back at college and they wouldn't be so busy. She liked it when the orders came fast as flies and you didn't have time to think. Then an air of organized hysteria hovered around the high grills and the steel topped tables.

Laurie got her writing paper out of the cabinet. My escritoire, she thought. The paper was a present from her nieces, chosen no doubt by Shelley. Sending her writing paper must mean they wanted her to carry on writing surely? She sat biting her pen, looking out at the high banked clouds.

Dear Brian and Shelley,
I'm feeling very restless tonight. Twitchy really. Why? Because I'm expecting my lover. Trouble is I only see him once a year, which I'm sure you'll agree is worse than useless. Sex once a year never did anybody any good. Have I shocked you Brian? Have I horrified you Shelley? I sincerely hope so. Who can this mystery man be? I shall tell you. Remember Malcolm, my erstwhile spouse? Well this is my erstwhile spouse's brother. That's right Brian. This is Jim. This affair, if you can call it an affair, has been going on for years. How scandalous! He's married of course and the family are based in the Middle East somewhere. (He got away too Brian, but further away than you.) Anyway Jim comes home

every year to see his mother in Liverpool. I suppose he goes over to Southport to see Malcolm and his tribe too, but I never ask him and he never tells me. That, Brian is called discretion.

It must have been very reassuring for you to think you had a sister back home who was a model of rectitude and moral propriety. Well she ain't, Brian. No way.

Hoping you're all keeping well,
Your loving sister,
Laurie.

Now that Laurie had flirted effectively with the letter she would *not* be writing she was able to concentrate on the matter in hand. She coughed. Cleared her throat. Managed to describe the poppies and next door's latest batch of kittens. A kindle of kittens, what a lovely phrase, but she wondered why Mrs. Kubicz didn't get the poor animal spayed. It looked worn out. For reassurance Laurie looked across the room at her own Minxie, still in the peak of condition, still a beautiful cat. What else could she add? Something about a nip in the air in the mornings, the blackberries ripening in the hedge. Did they have blackberries in Germany? Three quarters of an hour to go before she needed to leave for *The Saracen's*. Laurie propped the letter up on the mantlepiece, ready and waiting.

Then something strange happened. Minxie had a personality change. By nature phlegmatic, even staid, a cat not generally given to energetic outbursts of any kind, she suddenly became quite kittenish. To Laurie's astonishment she started to run backwards and forwards along the backs of the chairs and up on to the table in the window.

'Calm down Minxie,' said Laurie softly. 'What's the matter girl? Do you want to go out?' Minxie calmed down. She coiled her sinuous tabby markings decorously as she settled next to the Boston fern and its splendid fronds. If nothing else Laurie was good with plants.

If anyone had been observing the last in a row of long, thin houses that night they would have seen a white car park at the back, with some difficulty as there wasn't much room, and a tall balding man emerge from it. He passed Laurie's border where the ghostly remains of the decapitated poppies hissed drily, opened the little gate at the side and walked down the passage to the back door. The key was in its usual place in a tub of geraniums so he let himself in. He looked around him. Nothing had changed. He flicked through the paper. Still the same old news. By the time Laurie got back he'd made himself at home and was sat there with a bottle of wine and an adequate supply of the surplus charm with which he'd captivated her originally.

It was funny to think they were brothers. They weren't a bit alike. Malcolm had snored for a start. Whenever he rolled on to his back it would begin, the low rumble followed by the high pitched whine. Laurie couldn't stand it. She would try to push him over on to his side, the snores getting louder all the time. He was a dead weight. Then, eventually, when she'd solved that problem he'd start his diagonal take over bid. Laurie would end up in the cold third of the bed. Near the top on the left with nowhere to put her legs. Perched on the edge.

Laurie had to admire the way Jim always slept so neatly. Lying there in the early light she looked at his back, the mottled patches like spreading freckles on his shoulders, the mole at the base of his neck. She was sorry he was going bald. They'd both had such beautiful hair, but Malcolm's was thicker, more wiry. Was he going bald too? It was so artificial really, the way neither of them spoke about Malcolm at all. As if he didn't exist. Did they talk about her though? Compare notes? Laugh? They ought to laugh. The whole thing was stupid. Just once she'd like to be a fly on the wall. Just once, in Southport. She'd like to see what the children looked like. Not *her*. She didn't want to see *her*. But yes, she would have liked to see the children.

Laurie felt very calm. And sad. But sad in a calm way. Now that it was here, this moment, now that all the speeches she'd rehearsed were about to be put to the test she knew she wouldn't be able to say those things. Not the way she'd intended, anyway. She couldn't. And it wasn't as if she thought those things would hurt him. She didn't think it would hurt him. It might, she hoped, surprise him. Just a bit. He'd always been honest with her hadn't he?

Prided himself on it. He'd told her at the start he couldn't let things get complicated. Once before, when the pointlessness of it all had surfaced more sharply than usual, when she told him just how *used* he made her feel, he didn't seem to understand.

'I don't want to not see you again,' he'd said. And he looked so, well, earnest about it. Then, three years ago, that seemed to be enough.

'Jim,' she said quietly, snuggling up into his back, her mouth level with the mole, so she could, if she'd wanted to, bitten it clean off. 'I'm going to sell the house.'

He stirred and mumbled something. This was cowardice. Laurie sat up very slowly, pulling herself up very gently so she wouldn't disturb him. She looked down at his sleeping face. The creases seemed to have smoothed out of it. He looked, well, young. She remembered how, after their mother died, she would look in on Brian when he was asleep. To see that he was alright. To check he was breathing. He was eight then. She'd been thirteen. She had wanted him to be safe. And Malcolm. And Jim. She wanted them all to be safe.

But I don't want to see any of you again. Ever. She could hear traffic in the distance now. It was ten to six. She eased herself out of bed trying not to wake him.

'That you?' She turns as he moves towards her. Turns away. Guilty. He's rolled over on to his back now. Rubs his eyes. 'What's the time?' She tells him. 'Jim,' she starts again, bolder now. 'I'm going to sell the house.' I don't think he knows where he is. I'm sure he doesn't. I bet he thinks he's at home. 'It's me, Jim.'

'I know it's you.'

'I want to tell you something.'

'M'mm?'

'I'm selling up.' He's not properly awake. That's why I'm telling him now, because....

'What?'

'I won't be here anymore.'

'What are you doing there? Come back to bed. It's early.'

'I'm trying to tell you I'm selling the house.' He sits up now. Scrumples his hair so the thin strands stick out on top. It doesn't matter, Jim. Going bald I mean. It doesn't matter at all.

'What are you talking about Laurie?'

'I'm moving.'

Jim squints at her as if the sun's in his eyes. 'Where? Why?'

'I don't know where yet. It's just that I can't stand it here anymore.'

'And?'

'And what?'

'What are you saying really?'

'I don't want to see you again, Jim. But I'm not angry. At all. I don't want you to think I'm angry.'

'You don't look angry. Do you think you ought to look angry?'

'I'm not.'

'Alright. You should know.'

Jim props himself up on his elbows, leans back against the pillows. Looks at her. Not squinting at her now.

'Laurie,' he says. Very softly.

She shakes her head.

'O.K. If that's what you want.'

'It is. It's what I want.'

Laurie is trembling. She stands at the window, her hand finding the coolness of the poppy tin. She sees the steep road, the strips of yellow privet, the redbrick walls with their ridiculous crenellations. She sees them as a stranger might see them. She sees them for the first time.

The Last Thrush

Each evening the thrush would come. She would hear its click and thump, that sharp repeated sound, that hammer on the anvil. She could not see it. Lying here, how could she? But it was almost as if she could. See it. Be it. Be which of them though? There are two of them out there. Thrush and snail. And the air is warm and calm as the sound carries. It fills the room.

'Time for your medication, Mrs. Shone. Can you manage dear? Let me help you sit up. That's it....'

Her voice is too tired to move in the air that holds the sound of the thrush on the step. There it is again. Across the garden at the far end by the shed. The sound has travelled a long way to climb through the white window. And why should such a sound be comforting? It is a murderous sound. And yet there is a closeness to it. A familiar shape.

CLICK. Click. Click. Click. THUMP.

And the probing bill of the thrush scoops thickly, scoops thinly in the softness inside the shell.

Her own pain is misted but still there somehow. Constantly there in the background. Like water seeping slowly on a stone. Out there in the garden on the step of the shed the thrush declares itself. The Russian vine that half buries the shed shifts lightly like an animal in its sleep and moves its cream white flowers.

Dr. Whittaker called today. She smiled at him and the effort of the smile creased and set on her face. Is this what a death mask is? Is this what it means? How fond of him. She has grown so fond of him over the years. They are the same age. Yes, exactly. He'd just joined old Dr. Garnett's practice when she was expecting Stephen. Does he ever think about Stephen? Does he ever wonder what he might have been?

And when he asked her whether she felt she needed more of the painkiller, she found, for once, that her voice could be clean and strong. It was her voice. Her own. And she was proud, not so much of the words, their meaning, though that was important too, but of their clarity, their sureness. She was still here.

'No,' she said, pulling the words up from a cool place she still kept inside her. 'No. Really.' And the smile was stuck on her face though she wanted to move it. 'I don't need any more. I'm floating about as it is. As if I'm not properly here. As it is.'

He had smiled then, touched her lightly on the arm. And he was such a big man, clumsy really, though for all his awkwardness his touch was so *bright*. And she had wanted to thank him for the deep space he made in the room. A space for breathing. How did he feel about this, about her? They had grown old together, hadn't they? Isn't it strange? And yet they were neither of them old. Not *old*. Not really. She was a long way off growing *really* old. But what did growing old have to do with dying? With this?

Dr. Whittaker moved softly in the room. She saw him write the prescription. She saw him hand it to the nurse. She heard the click of his bag as it closed. And the click of that bag, so near, was somehow so much further away than that other click, that thump on the step outside. It was ridiculous. How could she possibly know what it was like, how it felt, to be a snail being slowly eaten by a thrush?

But she did know. She felt it. Perhaps God was like a thrush. Hammering. Pounding. Probing inside the human shell. Did she believe in God? Did she believe there was anything out there? In the end?

* * * * *

The agency nurse is young this time. Her name is Jenny. Not a particularly earnest name, perhaps. Jenny. But she is earnest. She is young and earnest and has large capable hands. Everything she does, every move she makes, is competent, is ordered and controlled. She takes a pride in this. But now, as she moves about the old-fashioned kitchen, and to get a new kitchen to look this old, this *natural* would cost you thousands, her thoughts are neither ordered nor controlled. She is thinking about Mark. What is she going to say to him? She reaches for one of those Greek yoghurts from the fridge. Creamy. Plain. Peels off the foil lid and stirs in a little honey the way Mrs. Shone likes it.

Mark, the way I feel at the moment I don't want to go to Switzerland with you. Yes, I know I've always said I wanted to go to Switzerland, and I have, ever since I was a child. And I was looking forward to it. But somehow, now, I just don't want to go.

Mrs. Shone never complains. I just wish her son would come to see her more often, that's all. He's been twice in five weeks. Fleeting visits. And now he's in France, covering the run-up to the elections, so I don't suppose he'll be back till that's over. I did think it would be quite something. To be able to say I'm nursing Michael Shone's mother. And he *is* just as good looking in real life as he is on T.V. It's costing him of course. All this. But I can't say I like him. And somehow I don't think she likes him either. Not really. In fact I'm sure she doesn't. That's stupid, I suppose. But there's always this awkwardness. I don't know....

Mark, I can't explain why I don't want to go on holiday with you. I look round this house and I see it through your eyes. *Distinctive country residence of great character set in mature gardens.*

And I don't want this woman to die.

* * * * *

She lies in her golden world. In the light from the window. She is not awake. She is not asleep. She is floating on a lake. Misty.

'Jenny? Are you there?'

'Yes, Mrs. Shone. I'm here.'

'What's the time?' Her lips are very dry. Crusted. Jenny gently dampens them.

'Half past five. Nearly'

'Has it come?'

'What? What's that Mrs. Shone? I didn't quite hear you.'

'The thrush.'

'M'mm?'

'Can you hear it? Listen. That click sound. There, I'm sure you heard it then. Did you?'

'I think I heard something. Yes.'

'Go and have a look, would you? It's on the step of the shed. Thrushes have always used that step, you know. And I've lived in this house for forty three years. How many thrushes is that, do you think? How many snails? Stephen brought me some snail shells one day, small and black with gold bands. Like enamel. I'd never seen any like that before. He was always finding things.'

'Stephen?'

Mrs. Shone closes her eyes. The lids are papery thin. Transparent.

'You don't know, do you?'

'Know what Mrs. Shone?'

'Just go and look for me, would you, Jenny. On the step of the shed. Please.'

* * * * *

At the side of the house there are two arches. One of roses. One of honeysuckle. The honeysuckle arch has come loose from the wall, the bracket rusted through. As the warm heavy wind rises, it scrapes and rasps against the wall. The kind of noise that strums in your head. Irritating. Repetitive. But this isn't Mrs. Shone's sound. It can't be. This is a noise not a sound. And the rest of the garden is hushed and sleepy with late summer and the small shift of branches. So what can it be?

CLICK. Click. Click. Click. THUMP.

Jenny follows this sharp new sound. To the shed. It is bathed in its Russian vine. Its delicacy, its leaves and cream white flowers, contradict the stained planks, the square window fixed with chicken wire.

And the thrush is there on the step. Sleek. Purposeful. Hammering then pausing then hammering again. First this way. Then that. Then plunging its bill into the hollow of the shell. Then looking up, its eye shining, a strand of liquid snail flesh glistening on the edge of its bill. And seeing her. Watching closely. But unafraid.

Unconcerned. Softly, as she stands there, with hardly a sense that it is about to move at all, it flies, unhurried, as if in slow motion, into the low slightly browning shape of the lilac.

'I'm so sorry Miss Dawson. I frightened you.'

'No, no. Not at all,' she says, turning, laughing. Then, 'Well, you did a bit, actually, Mr. Shone. I didn't know you were there. I didn't expect....'

'I've just got a couple of hours. I'll be flying back first thing in the morning. How is she?'

'No change, Mr. Shone. It can't be long now. Dr. Whittaker called again today. She said she didn't want any more of the medication.'

'She's not in pain?'

'No. I don'think so. But she's brave you know. Wants to stay alert. It's important to her. And I feel, perhaps I shouldn't say this, I think there's something she wants to tell me but doesn't quite know how.'

'What do you mean?'

'I wondered if you might know who Stephen is? She mentioned him.... A child I think. Something to do with snail shells.'

In the deep web of the garden with its scents and its quiet hidden murderousness, in the earth, in the bark of the trees, in the golden tent under the damson tree where spiders abseil against the trunk on single threads, there is a strange waiting quietness.

'He was my brother. Hasn't she mentioned him before?'

'I'm so sorry. I shouldn't have....'

'No, Miss Dawson. Please. It's hardly your fault, is it? And anyway, it was a long time ago.'

Michael Shone's voice bears the hallmark of urgent action. Incidents accompany it. World events authorise it. War. Famine. Earthquake. That distinctive tone. Does it fit in here? Now?

Jenny tries to turn them round. Turn them back towards the house. He won't let her. Not yet.

'He was drowned. Just a week before his seventh birthday. The pond isn't there any more. All that land went for the by- pass years ago.'

'You don't have to tell me. I feel I've intruded.'

'No. I think I should explain. You'll understand then. The distance. Between my mother and me. She never forgave me, you see. She kept everything. His toys. His clothes.' He smiles a strange smile that is both vivid and closed. 'And his snail shells. An ammonite. A piece of amber with a fly in it. Rusty nails. He said they were Roman. That was after some excavations in the fields behind the church. My father was away a lot so it was up to me. It was so morbid. One Christmas, I was ten, I got everything together in boxes and sacks. And I sank them. In the pond. Seemed the best thing to do, but she was so crazy, so, well, demented, when she found out I thought she'd go in after them. It was terrible. She didn't, thank God, but it was what you might call the end of a beautiful friendship. So you see Miss Dawson, there's usually a simple explanation for these things. Don't you agree?'

Jenny looks up at his face. She looks for the hurt child that must surely, still be there. She can't find him.

'I think we should go in now Mr. Shone. Your mother actually sent me out to look for the thrush. I don't know what I'm supposed to say to her.'

'I should think you were meant to find something, don't you? Black shells with yellow rings on them? Well, you haven't, have you?'

Upstairs in the steep house Mrs. Shone carries on with her dying. Now it's on a higher note. And in a different key. The celestial thrush that is the God she can't believe in is standing by the window. He's blocking out most of the light. He's huge. Glossy. Wiping his great bill on the top of the dressing table mirror. And now Jenny's come back. Where has she been? And now Michael. Why is he here? How strange it is.

In their nest in the lilac tree a late brood of thrush fledglings thrust their soft bright mouths into the air. On the step of the shed the litter of snail shells gathers. Cinnamon fragments as the light catches them. Mosaic splinters. But mostly plain snail grey.

Pink Summer Blues

L ast night I knew they knew. Just as soon as I saw Daz and his mob at the end of the street. They'd already seen me. If they hadn't, I could've sneaked down the path at the side of Snips and got home that way. Too late. I made myself walk tall and slow.

'Hey, look who it isn't.'

'It's that stuck up kid. Yer know, wot's 'er name.'

'Used to talk to us, didn't she? Thinks she's too good for us now. Stuck-up cow.'

I had to look at them, but with what sort of face? That stupid nerve in my cheek started twitching.

Daz was half sat, half slumped on the rail outside the chip shop. I concentrated inside and willed him not to get up on his feet. They'd take their cue from him. As long as he stayed relaxed, kind of casual like that, sneering but not really threatening, I might be O.K.

'Hafwen!' he shouted as I passed. Then straightaway he looked sideways at Gary. 'That her name, Gaz? It's something funny like that.'

'Yeah. Hafwen. Welsh, innit?'

'And what's her sister called?' I groaned deep down. So they knew alright.

'Leri, yeah?'

They were all laughing. Daz spoke very slowly, his voice heavy with mock concern. 'I've heard she's landed herself in a spot of bovver.'

'Something like that.'

He was looking straight at me. Dead sarcastic and cool. I didn't want to but I had to admire the way he handled it.

'You wouldn't believe it, would you? I mean, they're such a *respectable* family.'

'But it's political, innit?'

'What's that, Gaz?'

'Well, second homes and protests. Welsh nationalists and that.'

'What's she done then?'

'Got into that new estate agent's in town and smashed the computers or something. Her and some of her mates. Then phoned the police to say they'd done it.'

'No.'

'Yeah.'

'She's in college, isn't she?'

'You'd think she'd know better, wouldn't you? I mean, educated and that.'

'Yeah, you would.'

They were enjoying this. Making a meal of it. Then the expression on Daz's face changed.

'You know what gets me about this, Gaz. Really pisses me off I mean, cos, you know how I hate injustice.' There was a buzz of relish all around.

'What's that?'

'If it was you and me did this, something like this, we'd get it wouldn't we? We'd go down. The works. We'd cop the lot. Breaking and entering. Criminal damage. She won't, you know.'

'How d'you reckon that?'

'Well, like you said, it's political. Different, isn't it?'

The words were out before I realised. 'It'll be treated just the same,' I said. 'She'll be charged just the same.' My face was burning, all the more as I realised I'd walked right into it. Just as he'd planned. 'She'll go to court and she'll probably go to prison. That's what she expects.'

'And wants? Wants to be a martyr? That's what it's all about, isn't it?' Then he looked away from me and back at his gang again. It was like he was conducting an orchestra. 'Hey listen, you lot. Did you hear that? She can still talk when she wants to. She can still manage it. Didn't think you could, Hafwen. Thought you'd forgotten. How to speak English, I mean.'

I stared at him. My legs wanted to run, but the rest of me wanted to stay. Fight if necessary. But whose side was I on anyway? And it wasn't as if I even liked Leri half the time. And anyway Daz wasn't English. He wasn't proper Welsh either, not like my family, but you couldn't say he was English. And I was tired. My feet were aching. I felt sticky and the sweet stink of candy floss was stuck in my clothes, my hair. I could do without this. All of it.

Then, it was as if I was moving up on a sliding scale of anger, he said something that just finished me off.

'D'you know some thing, Gaz. She's not got bad legs, has she? Always got that bloody serious expression on her face, though. Puts you off.'

'Yeah,' said Gaz. 'Studious type.'

I wanted to hit them. Flatten them. But my anger just made me pathetic. They knew they'd got me riled and that inspired them all the more. Daz had a special line in sarcasm, and part of me, I had to admit, wanted to laugh. There'd been a poor supply of laughter in our house ever since Leri'd got into the language act and my mother was flopping round the house having nervous breakdowns all the time.

Now he was grinning all over his face. 'If she's not careful she'll be going off to college like her sister and smashing computers too. D'you think there's a special course in it, Gaz? Can anyone get on it? What about us? I wouldn't mind a diploma in smashing computers, but they wouldn't call it that, would they?'

'No. They'd make it sound better than that. Something like computer demobilization....'

'Right! How about Computer Demobilization and Sabotage?'

I didn't know what to say. Or do. And I couldn't just creep away either. I was like a mesmerised rabbit. The rest of the gang was getting bored with it by now. They started shuffling their feet and a couple of them lit up. Little Andy Patterson started to blow smoke rings.

Sensing that this particular line of entertainment had run out of steam, Daz wound it up. He picked himself up from his perch and seemed to glide off with that peculiar drifting walk of his. The others followed with hardly a backward glance, except for Gary, who looked as if there was more he wanted to say. It's weird, but left standing there I felt kind of lost. Was this the sort of kick Leri got out of her antics? I was just going to sidle off myself when Daz turned round and shouted, dead loud so everyone in the estate could hear, 'When's it coming up in court then?'

'I don't know,' I mumbled, ashamed of my feeble-sounding voice.

'I want to be kept informed,' he said, nudging Gary. 'I want to be kept up to date with the latest developments.'

And at last I managed to show a bit of life. 'Of course,' I said, as if I'd been a student at Daz's very own school of street cred. 'I'll make certain you get regular bulletins. Watch this space.'

And when they'd disappeared round the corner at last, the street looked so dull and dead.

* * * * *

I know I moan and groan about this job but I like it really. I like the whirr and hum the drum makes as it turns. Pouring the hard shiny crystals of sugar into the funnel thing in the middle is good too. I can't explain why, but there's something really satisfying about measuring out those shocking pink grains. Perhaps it's the way they glitter. Like rubies, I don't know. And I love the look on the kids' faces. It's a kind of magic to them and, though I ought to be used to it by now, there's still something special about the way the thin strands appear suddenly on the sides of the drum. Like whisps of pink mist. I collect it, sweep it up on the stick in clouds that get bigger and thicker. And if there's a kid I particularly like the look of, I give it an extra twirl.

The other good thing about this job (well, let's face it, any job) is it gets me out of the house. And it's funny now with all this trouble with Leri and everything, my Mum doesn't keep going on about selling candy floss being common like she did when I started. She didn't approve at all. But I don't think it's got anything to do with candy floss really. She just doesn't want to admit we're grown up. And I'm the baby. The last one. For her growing up means going away like John did. Though I've told her not to worry. I've got no intention of going to Saudi!

It's awful at home. Dad is always quiet anyway, but if he's not at work he's in the garden with his sweet peas and his gladioli, keeping out of the way. He just won't talk about it and that makes Mum worse. I'm sorry for her but what can I do? Leri's not in much. She spends most of her time with that Iestyn.

Mum hates him. He's got all this long black hair and beard and he's a drummer in this weird Welsh band. She says if it hadn't been for him Leri would never have got mixed up with the language lot in the first place. That's not true. All the others are with her in college and she knew them long before she ever met Iestyn.

When Leri is around she acts like she's a princess or something. Says we ought to be proud of her and the stand she's making. I think Mum is proud of her. In a way. She's from Tre Taliesin and you can't get more Welsh than that. Dad always says she never really settled here though he kept hoping that she would, sooner or later. The fact that she named Leri after the river that ran at the bottom of their garden shows how homesick she was, I suppose. She's never really comfortable when she's speaking English. You can tell. But she's such a timid little person. Scared of her own shadow. And all this business with the police coming to the house and everything, it's made her that she won't go out at all and she hides behind the curtains if someone comes to the door.

As for me I'd respect Leri more if she didn't seem to love being the star of the show. I don't think she's genuine. Some of the others are. Definitely. I've listened to them talk and they've got it all worked out. They've thought it through, this business of sabotaging the computer links in the estate agents. They know what they're doing and why. Sometimes I wish I could be like that. Clear minded. Committed. Sure you're right. Leri says it's people like her that get things done. I wish I could really believe it's possible to change things. The language is important. I know that. And it's not just a question of different words for the same things. A language makes you think and feel in a special way. It makes you what you are.

But I can't help feeling it's a kind of game for Leri. She'd like to be a film star, something like that, and this is second best. Still, I'm prejudiced. I admit it. I think it would be much better if she went to Saudi and John came back.

Last night Mum started crying very quietly to herself. I sat by her on the sofa and tried to give her a hug but she only pushed me away. So I went to look for Dad in the garden. I keep telling him Mum's getting worse all the time and he really ought to do something about it. I don't know what though. She won't go the doctor's and she won't have him come to the house. I said to Leri when she came in just to collect a dress she wanted, doesn't she ever think about the effect she's having on Mum? Leri said she was just neurotic and had always been the same. Which is true, I suppose, but so cold, so uncaring. She's like that.

It's huge, our garden. Iestyn says you could build two bungalows at least in it, but Dad bought it for the garden as a garden, not as a building site. It's the last bungalow before the Pwll y Maen estate which used to be quite nice but is awful now with half the houses boarded up and the gardens full of old cars propped up on bricks. Anyway, I stood at the top of the path and looked down towards the sea and all the lights blinking along the bay. Down there somewhere is my stripey booth with the sweet sickly smell I'm sure I'll be carrying round in my nose for the rest of my life. And then I realised something.

I like my job because it's mindless. Stops me thinking about all the trouble at home. And stops me thinking about my results. They'll be out in two weeks time. I don't think I've done too badly and I'm sure I've done O.K. in the ones I'm going to go on with. Welsh, French and English. Like Leri.

I wonder how Daz has got on. He's clever really and he used to be great when we were in primary school. I won't be telling him Leri's court hearing's on Monday. He'll be able to read all about it in The Gazette anyway. Poor Mum. It'll kill her, that. Knowing everybody will be reading about it. I sometimes wish I could talk to Daz in an ordinary sort of way. He's alright really under all that stupid act he has to put on for the others.

It's all an act isn't it? Life, I mean. I know Dad's down there in the tool shed. He's sharpening something. I can hear the whetstone going.

As I come down the steps it's starting to get really dark. The sun is just about to dip down in the waves, making a glitter on the water. I just wish things were different. I wish there was something I could do to make it better. If I had enough money I'd take Mum away for a holiday. Somewhere peaceful and quiet.

But you can't get away from yourself, can you?

Life Isn't Like That

E ven now, after all these days of slow pale heat the moss in the wall was still spongy. Jill poked the thin green cushion with her finger. The moss flowers, the tiny threads, were flattened, sinking back into the crevice between the bricks, oozing moisture on the rough surface.

'It's in the wall,' he said. 'Look. This isn't just damp. Can't be.'

And he'd taken a knife from his pocket then, something like a penknife, surprisingly delicate, with a handle of mother of pearl.

'There,' he said. 'See.'

And he'd scraped away the moss. Not just there. Here, too. And here. She felt the sharpness as the vivid green wads sliced from the cracks, the curls falling softly on the concrete.

'Saturated,' he said. 'There's water seeping from inside somewhere.' Now he ran his finger along the gaps. 'This mortar's gone. Sopping. All of it. It's a hairline crack in a pipe I'd say.' He turned to face her. 'It's the original lead piping I suppose?'

Jill half shrugged, half shook her head. She didn't know.

'And there's no cavity wall either?'

'No,' said Jill. Her voice was like a glum bell that didn't want to ring. She couldn't claim for any of this on the small insurance she'd finally persuaded Paul to take out. This was wear and tear. The house was old, the back wall taking the brunt of winter, the wind from the sea clenched with salt so your lips were caked with it.

'Like a slow puncture in a tyre.'

It was as if he was talking to himself now. As if she wasn't there. He kept prizing between the bricks. Efficiently. Objectively. For him these were facts. Just facts.

My house is falling down, thought Jill.

'You've not lived here long, have you?'

69

'Three years. Nearly.'

'You got a survey done on the place before you bought it?'

She wanted to say it wasn't my idea. It was Paul's. Leap first. Think after. Then, when you've seen the mess you've made, walk out on it. Let someone else pick up the pieces. And I don't even know where he is. But she said none of these things.

'No,' she said.

The silence between them made a sound of its own, like a slithering through a strainer. He didn't know what to say.

'It's going to cost a lot, isn't it?' she helped him.

'Tell you what I'll do. I'll break the estimate down, right? And I'll get hold of a plumber to trace the leak. He's a good bloke. Won't rip you off. Then there's all that loose brickwork under the sill....'

Jill bit her lip. 'Thank you,' she said.

* * * * *

Saturday morning. She woke early, moved softly downstairs so as not to wake the girls. She wanted time to herself. This was the best part of the day, or used to be. The sky washed new, the quietness, the air unbreathed by anyone. She opened the kitchen door, found herself standing very stiff, very upright. She would face it. She had to. It was getting worse. The damp, whatever it was, those flurried patterns, those cloud shapes, was spreading. It began with dark new blobs against the flaking plaster, then, growing all the time, these became the palm of a hand, its tapering fingers. It was inside the fabric. Eating them up.

How am I going to pay for this?

She stepped outside. Stretched fiercely. Breathed in. Heat haze again. A grey bright glare that made you screw up your eyes. I thought this was what he wanted. This place. I thought he'd be happy here. And now he could be dead for all I know. Why doesn't he write or something? Why doesn't he just let me know where he is?

Paul's debris was everywhere, reminding her. And in the back room, most of all his place, she could hardly bear to see the kiln, the pots in serried rows that people admired so much but seldom bought, the stacked canvases. Why did he go like that, without a word? But wasn't that a stupid question? She knew the answer, and it said as much about her, her own frailties, as it did about Paul. Earth mother. Dreaming artist. The clichéd roles they'd played to perfection. He'd never grown up. Never would, and that, paradoxically, was why she'd loved him. Past tense? No, she still loved him. But what about the girls? What in practical terms was she supposed to do now?

Then Connie, mouse-quiet, was there, pulling at her crumpled nightie, rubbing the sleep from her eyes.

'Effie's only got one eye now, mummy. Look. She's lost the other one. That means she can only half see now, doesn't it?'

'I've got it safe,' said Jill. 'I found it on the floor by your bed when I was tucking you up, remember? We can sew it on again can't we?'

The threadbare elephant flopped forgotten on the table and Connie reached up, her small hands stars on her mother's shoulders. Jill lifted her with a swoosh, rubbing her face against the child's hot fine hair.

'What are we going to do, mummy? Can we go somewhere?'

'I'll see.'

'You said we could go on a picnic.'

'Did I?'

'Yes. You did say. You did promise, mummy.'

'Oh no I didn't.' Jill was laughing. 'Anyway, terror, is Sophie up yet?'

'No. She's a lazy bones, isn't she?'

'You go and get dressed, right? Hang on, let's give you a lick and a promise.' She dampened the corner of a kitchen towel and wiped the morning face till it shone. 'What do you want in your sandwiches?'

'We are going!'

'Only if you both hurry up so we can catch the bus. Would you like cheese spread?'

'No. Proper cheese. And pickles in it for Sophie but I don't like pickles. And green jam.'

'Green jam?'

'That Nana brought.'

'Oh, the gooseberry. I didn't think you liked it.'

'Sophie can have it.'

'She can, can she? Listen, bossy boots, Sophie may stay in bed longer than you but she can get a move on, can't she? She knows how to hurry when she has to. What does Nana call you?'

'Dilly Dawdle.' Connie was giggling now, retrieving the elephant and sucking its one remaining half chewed ear.

'Get up those stairs then, Dilly Dawdle.' Jill closed her eyes and sighed, listening to the clattering on the bare boards, followed by yelling and muffled thumps. Then came Sophie's sharp voice and the slam of the bathroom door.

We'll go to St. David's, she told hersef. That's what we'll do. We'll get the early bus and make a day of it. She grabbed some bruised apples from the fruit bowl, a packet of biscuits from the cupboard. There were only two yoghurts left. Never mind. One peach, one strawberry.Then she started on the sandwiches, seeing, was it only last year, the four of them sat on the cliffs among linnets and furze. A certain quality of light, a luminosity Paul always tried to capture in his paintings, bathed everything around them, highlighting every detail with a sharp edged clarity. Beyond them always was the steady murmur of the sea. How different she'd felt then. How completely at peace with herself and the world. She saw the foxgloves by the well, the layered purple rock in Caerfai Bay, and Paul, laughing, tickling Sophie's feet with curls of fern.

She blinked determinedly, wrestling with the lid of the pickle jar.

* * * * *

I am not unhappy, thought Mr. Kyrle.

Sheba padded softly behind, nosing among blown crisp packets and yellowed summer grass, living in her coded world of smells. Some were reassuring and familiar, others rare and strange. She was disturbed by these. Mr. Kyrle detected a tremor cross her smooth flank. We're not so different, he thought. We only feel safe with what we know. Hostility to change, to difference, dogs feel it too, unless they're young of course. And life is an adventure. Sheba, in canine terms, was a nonagenarian. What was he?

They found their place, the seat perched in the elbow of the zig-zag. Behind them burnt gorse scarred the slope. Whitened stumps reared up from the charred tangle, reminding him of building husks on a bomb site, the aftermath of the blitz in Manchester. Why did his mind play these tricks on him? Images he'd prefer to forget kept surfacing unbidden. Where did the gentler memories go?

Sheba was nudging persistently at his left leg, bringing him back in her stubborn way. Sit down, she kept telling him. Come on. We're here, aren't we? So he sat, and she, breathing wheezily, settled at his feet, her head placed squarely on her paws. 'Good girl,' he whispered, tickling her behind the ears, vowing to himself that once her quality of life was threatened he'd have her put to sleep. Quality of life? What a phrase! What was Edith's, God help her, at the end?

The haze hid the little harbour and the boats at rest. The tide was out, leaving the shallow brown river to find its own way to the sea, and there, as ever, half tucked into the hillside, but leaving that one exposed shoulder, was the house. He felt the usual twin pull of love and hate. Was this becoming an obsession? Was it morbid, walking here every day? To deliberately set out not to come this way would be just as bad though, wouldn't it? He didn't know. It wasn't in his nature to avoid the unpleasant, any more than seek it. He took life as it came. Or had done. But he'd never experienced anything like this before. This sense of being totally rudderless. Without purpose. Without direction. Drifting. His working days had been full, but he'd looked forward to their long planned retirement. He and Edith had shared many interests. It would be making a dream come true, to retire to Pembrokeshire....

That very first time they'd come here, before they were married, and that, a cycling holiday, just the two of them, was considered quite daring in those days, the house had beckoned them immediately, standing alone in its wild garden with its shining view of harbour and headland and moody sea. 'Live in me,' it had said, and they, young, in love, and eagerly romantic had responded,

'Yes. One day. We will, we will.'
But life isn't like that.

Sheba started to snore and then twitched in her sleep, startling herself awake. 'It's alright girl,' he said softly. Did dogs dream? They seemed to. Did that mean they had some sort of unconscious? He focused his attention on the cliffs opposite, the white gulls floating. It was strange weather. So still. And everything was neutralised somehow, by this grey filtered sunlight. Above the house you could see the pines waiting for the wind, the shifting air that shaped them. But there was no air moving at all. Not here. It was thick this air, this a slab of stillness.

He was too restless to sit for long, setting off again, a reluctant Sheba in tow. 'You're getting lazy, old girl,' he said, aware of the false cheeriness in his voice. What a pathetic sight they made, the pair of them. Widower walks with his dog. He saw his actions captioned. Lampooned. Back home again to his bungalow, its neatness, its order. Familiar things and framed photographs. One of Edith, a favourite, taken just after they'd moved in. Before the diagnosis. Before they knew. The others of the children; the daughter, married now and living in Vancouver, the son on his graduation day. He envisaged these images deliberately as he passed the sea house, looking away towards the town, its huddle of roofs.

Then, just at the point where the sweep of the coastal path met the drive, that woman appeared with those two small girls. He'd seen them before, of course. Edith, in particular, had been curious about the family. What were they like? Were they happy? She'd hoped they were, making up stories about them, imagining that one day, just by chance, she'd bump into that young woman somewhere, shopping maybe, tell her that almost forty years ago their house was her guiding star, her ideal, her perfection. Perhaps she'd be able to see inside. What was the view like from inside? How silly it all was, he thought. Really. And yet how important.

He hadn't seen the man lately. Hippy type. An endangered species, you might say, but somehow, here, not in the least incongruous. Set himself up as a potter or an artist, something along those lines. Opened a little studio. But by then Edith was ill. The old dream of the sea house stopped being an entertaining game. He learned it was best not to mention it. Funny, he couldn't remember when he'd seen the man last. Must've been last winter. A bitter cold day and there he was wearing a thin red shirt, the wind billowing in it. A kind of gesture. At that moment Mr. Kyrle had been raw in his grief. And his anger. The man's flamboyance, the stagey inappropriate clothes, had riled him. A phoney. That's what he was.

Now, remembering the way he'd felt then, the intensity of his own sudden, quite irrational hatred, he felt embarrassed, hung back on the path, so he wouldn't have to draw near, wouldn't have to face the young woman, turning away, looking down at Sheba. Anything.

So he didn't see the child fall. One minute there'd been three of them; the woman, harrassed looking, shouting at them, telling them to hurry. It was the smaller, somehow sturdier little one that was dragging behind. Then the thump and the yelling and the blood. He couldn't disappear now. He had to do something, say something.

She sat there in the rough gravel, a gaping hole in her knee.

'Oh Sophie,' the mother said, kneeling beside her, whipping a handkerchief from somewhere, trying, ineffectively, to staunch the blood. And all the time the crying fit to burst.

'Can't we go on our picnic now?' came a small voice with a whine in it.

'Don't be so selfish, Connie. Can't you see Sophie's hurt herself?'

And he stood looking down at them, surprised, as the woman looked up at him. She was not as young as he'd thought. It was the long hair, the clothes she wore, those long Indian cottons — they'd given the illusion of youth. No. There were creases, yes, wrinkles round her eyes, and an air of what...such sadness, something pleading, yet proud and pained. He couldn't say what it was. He felt well, strange. Helpless. The look passed over her face and was gone, replaced by a conventional closed politeness.

'I think she'll need stitches in that, you know. It's a nasty cut.'

Again the woman's face clouded and now the second child started to cry, ashamed, perhaps of her earlier outburst. What a desperate little trio they made.

'Look,' he said. 'I live nearby. I'll get the car. She can't walk to the surgery like that. Just stay here and wait....'

'No, really....'

'I insist. I won't be long....'

And there was Sheba padding along after him. A moment of inspiration. 'No Sheba, you can stay here. You can guard these ladies till I get back.'

The dog looked up at him. 'Stay,' he said firmly. Then she looked at her charges. Understood. Wagged her tail. It was magic, the effect. Half the crying stopped immediately. And even the injured party was almost silenced.

'You're really very kind...' said Jill.

Mr. Kyrle was off at quite a gallop up the path. He looked back for a moment. Connie was hugging the patient, placid Sheba. The mother was attending to the knee, rearranging the sodden hand-kerchief.

He felt strangely alive. And strangely important.

I am not unhappy, thought Mr. Kyrle.

Shall we Simulate the Polka?

Monday night was nightmare night. 'Mum,' I'd say, my voice strangely calm, 'where are the tubes to take away the sick?'

'Go back to bed,' came the whisper. 'It's all right. You're all right Meryn.'

Go back to bed Meryn did too. No lonely vigil on the cold landing thankyou. But it was not all right. And wouldn't be. What's more, Dad's voice would sheer through the fitful halo from the street. 'What the hell's the matter with her now?'

Three o'clock. Four o'clock. Gestapo time. And Dad turning loudly in the high bed. A beached whale perhaps. Better, an unexploded bomb hypnotically ticking. And Meryn, even a somnambulist Meryn, knew that tubes to take the sick away were somehow safer.

'Some of us have got to get to work in the morning,' came a rising grunt, and then a shuuuush, shuuush, shuush from the quieter half of the bed. Soft waves on pebbles.

It's all right for you, Dad. Some of us have got Miss Lord.

* * * * *

Miss Lord was one of the old fascist school. There've been so many subtle developments on the fascist front since then, it seems now, looking back, that her particular variety was almost reassuring in its simplicity. But I'd never come across anything like her. I couldn't compare.

She sent out such ripples of terror they started to reach out and touch me as early as Friday evening, so by Monday night it was high octane.... And Tuesday was Cookery too. The Devastating

Juggling Act....

How did the others do it? Carry it all, I mean. The big biscuit tin for starters. Why does memory make it always something sloshy like baked custard, that, on the way home, you just *have* to keep upright. Satchel of course, full of text books (there were text books in those days) and exercise books that *had* to stay in the satchel because my duffle bag let in the wet. And the sacred weapon, the hockey stick itself, boots anchored with an inefficient granny knot.

Spit it out and it might go away. What sadist devised that timetable? Tuesday. 1A. A single lesson of Gym in the morning, last lesson before dinner (invariably mince, mash, and a compote of swede and carrot, followed by semolina with a blob of jam. I ate the jam). And double something in the afternoon.

Now gym in the morning wasn't *that* bad. At least you knew where you were with the box and the horse and the ropes and the wall bars, the medicine ball (interesting name that) the rubber mats and the trampoline (tiny, so if you missed your footing you found yourself falling backwards and banged your head on the floor). At least you knew where you were. On the floor.

But double something in the afternoon could be anything. Seasonal details apart, it could mean Ho Ho Hockey when I spent my time slithering around at left back and trying to keep away from the ball. It could be No No Netball when I tried to borrow glory by passing to Lanky who always managed to ram it in with a deft flick of her large wrist. It could be tennis where I was occasionally successful, taking great pride whenever I managed to serve the ball over the net.

Worst of all it could be dancing in the hall.

* * * * *

And here I was at my son's wedding; a fraught emotional time, let's face it, for any mother, when I saw her. No, not Miss Lord. She, I imagine, has long since departed to that great hockey field in the sky. No, the person who appeared out of the tremulous champagne-induced haze was none other than Anita Mullen-Jones, Victrix Ludorum, queen of the long jump, star of the show.

I recognised her immediately, and sure enough, she recognised me. The intervening years, all thirty of them, just blurred away. We were back. Back in the changing rooms in the white scented smoke of Black Rose talcum powder, Jennifer Lakey in the manic middle of it, and Miss Lord, the avenging angel herself, bearing down upon our tearful giggles (we knew what was coming) in a healthy glow of righteous indignation. Anita had the grace to look embarrassed, if only momentarily. She always had style.

'Delightful wedding,' she said, 'You must be very proud. I didn't realise you were Simon's mother.'

'They make a charming couple, don't they?' I burbled. 'Susan's such a pretty girl. You know the family well?'

'Oh yes. Tanya and I were at college together. My daughter, she's over there, the girl in green, was born within days of Susan. They've always been such chums too. Isn't it extraordinary?'

'What?' I said, feeling mellow, which was pleasant, but also more than slightly stupid, which was not.

'Our meeting like this. D'you know I was only thinking yesterday about school. The happiest days of our lives! They don't make teachers like that anymore, do they?'

'No, thank God.' My enthusiasm was perhaps excessive, but blasts from the past, the unexpected ones, always get me that way. Already I'd smiled myself silly at all my ex in-laws for Simon's sake. The strain was beginning to tell.

'Remember Miss Lord?'

'How could I forget?'

'D'you remember how she hauled me out for not being able to do the polka? She was such a cruel bitch. Such a mocker.'

'Mocker? Of you, surely not,' I said unguardedly. 'Not our Victrix Ludorum!'

'I had to be Victrix Ludorum. I was too terrified to be anything else! Surely you remember? It was pouring with rain and it was the boys' turn for the gym so there we were in the hall, quaking in our plimsolls. Now, Sir Roger de Coverley I could just about manage, but the polka! I had no sense of rhythm at all. Not like you.'

'Me?' I said. 'Rhythm?'

'Yes. You could do it! Your feet just tickled the floor!'
Was this genuine? I looked at her hard over the top of my glass.
Fair play, Anita Mullen-Jones had never been a bitch, had she? Just
sickeningly good at games. That was quite bad enough.
'Could I do the polka?' I asked, incredulous.
'Of course you could. She never hauled you out, did she?'
'No,' I said. 'She just ignored me.' Then, with a shudder I added,
'I was beneath her contempt.'
'We were all beneath her contempt.' The princess of the parallel
bars stared out into the distance with an air of strange wistfulness.
Weddings do have the most peculiar effect on people. I found
myself looking at the crows' feet round her eyes. Our own
wrinkles creep up on us slowly, giving us time to adjust. But the
girl alongside me was somehow still there, the mask of her ageing
apart. 'I'm divorced too, by the way,' she said quietly. Then it was
back to school with a jolt of relief, that link of shared experience.
'One thing you could say about our Miss Lord. She was equally
horrible to everyone. No teacher's pets for her.'
'No,' I said. And then I remembered. There we were in the hall,
the rain snivelling copiously down the tall windows, the chairs all
stacked around the edges, and Miss Lord's lashing tongue excori-
ating all of us above the scratchy sound of the record, that incon-
gruously lavish, supposedly exhilarating music. Yes, that was it.
The polka. I could hear it.
'EIGHT STEPS. EIGHT STEPS! COME ALONG GIRLS. THIS IS
HOPELESS! YOU'RE PATHETIC! YOU, YES I'M POINTING AT
YOU. STEP OUT! STEP OUT AT ONCE!'
And sure enough I see the ashen face of Anita Mullen-Jones as
she obediently steps out and looks up at her. In a state of abject
terror she is too. And although I'd seen it that day I hadn't *really*
seen it. I was far too terrified to see anything, and far too egocentric
in my dread to register someone else's suffering. Above all, I
couldn't believe that someone as good at games as Anita was
really capable of invoking the ogre's wrath. But could I do the
polka? Really?
'I hated the dancing in the hall more than anything else,' I said,
in a sudden confessional gush. 'I hated games altogether but she

was always worse in the hall, wasn't she?'

'I think she hated music. It must've been something like that. She used to screw up her face when she shouted. I can see her now.'

So could I. 'Yes, it could've been something to do with the music. We might almost have enjoyed it in different circumstances, mightn't we? And she couldn't have that. Mostly though I think she simply hated *us*.'

'I wonder why though,' Anita mused. She's got a nice, open sort of face, I found myself thinking, rather to my surprise. Why had I never seen it before? 'D'you remember that very first lesson we had with her?'

'You bet. I had nightmares after it.'

'Our second day in the place, nervous little first-formers, quite scared to death, and her barking away. "INTO YOUR KIT GIRLS. COME ALONG. COME ALONG. FASTER THAN THAT. NOW OUT OF YOUR KIT. I WANT THIS DONE IN LESS THAN THREE MINUTES AND YOU WON'T GET OUT OF HERE UNTIL YOU DO." '

I started to laugh. She was brilliant!

'"INTO YOUR KIT! HURRY UP! HURRY UP! THREE MINUTES OR LESS! WE'LL CARRY ON TILL I'M SATISFIED. OUT OF YOUR KIT. THIS IS NOT GOOD ENOUGH. FASTER THAN THIS! YOU, THAT GIRL WITH THE GLASSES, CAN'T YOU FASTEN YOUR LACES? THIS IS SUPPOSED TO BE A GRAMMAR SCHOOL! I'VE NEVER SEEN GIRLS SO SLOW. INTO YOUR KIT! FASTER! COME ALONG! I WANT YOU TO UNDERSTAND ONE THING. ONE THING FROM THE START. I WON'T TOLERATE SLOPPINESS IN MY LESSONS. OUT OF YOUR KIT!" The more I think about it the more I'm convinced. That woman was sick.'

I sank into a heap of exhausted delight. 'Effective though. She got through to us, didn't she? We certainly understood.'

'She was an inspiration in a way. An object lesson in reverse. I was determined I'd be as different from her as anyone could possibly be.'

'What did you do when you left?'

81

'P.E. of course. Loughborough. Surprised?'

'No. You were so *good*. And after all, the teachers we had when she left were O.K. weren't they? Miss Staples, she was nice...'

'Yes, and she married Mr. Connop, remember? Geography?'

'Oh yes. Yes, I'd forgotten that. Isn't it strange though? First impressions. Mention "games mistress" and that's what I see. Our very own Miss Lord. The archetype.'

'The caricature. Almost too bad to be true.'

* * * * *

That night I couldn't sleep. Too much to eat. To drink. And too much excitement, all tinged with sadness. Simon — the first fledgling flown. The effort of doing it right. The falsity of that social balancing act.

And I think of Miss Lord. And Anita. And me doing the polka. Perhaps I really was doing the polka after all! I couldn't believe I could do anything right, even remotely right, within a hundred miles of our very own fascist extraordinaire!

I'd forgotten it. Had I? Until she brought it back. Tamed it, made it ludicrous. And the rhythm of it still shrills through my head. SHALL WE... SIM - U - LATE... THE POLKA... ON A TUESDAY AFT - ER - NOON.... Round and round it goes. EIGHT STEPS GIRLS! Come along girls. Faster, faster. FASTER!

The Medlar Tree

He brings her a cup of tea. Sweet. Milky. His own is strong. No milk. No sugar. It strikes him how odd this is. Shouldn't it be the other way round? They make a strange pair. He knows this. Likes the effect it makes. Moves carefully across the bustling room with the plastic beakers. Awkward. Too full. Hot in his hand. She looks up for a moment. Her face, creased in concentration, opens. Perhaps like a flower. Perhaps the slight unevenness of her teeth is the unevenness of petals. He sits beside her. Everything is very clear. The smear on the window has a rainbow in it.

Joan, the occupational therapist, the older one, is wearing a pale lemon cardigan. Fluffy wool like a baby's jacket. The buttons are the same colour. Patterned. Elliptical. She starts to dislodge twine on the seat of a stool some patient has got hopelessly entangled. He notices her hands are stubby fingered, very white. It's as if he's come out of the dark. He catches the eye of the charge nurse. The one he likes. David. He notices one of the blue epaulettes on his white coat needs a stitch in it. It's coming loose.

Bev is busy. How different her hands are. Rough looking skin, like the beginnings of eczema. Flaky. She bites her nails. Ugly. But they're vivid hands. Scrabbly, like a little animal's. A vole or a field mouse. He knows she's glad he's brought her tea. That he's sitting alongside her. Makes her safe. She's setting her mosaic pieces in the cement, very steadily. She's chosen the ones that are flecked with green. It's a deeper green than the ribbon he's winding round the frame. For the shade. It will be good when it's finished. They will have made it together. The base and the shade. Whose will it be then? He smiles inside.

'Julian?'

'Yes.'

'What do you think?'

"I think it's fine. It looks fine.'

She sips at her tea. When he first saw her he was afraid of her. Her spiky hair. A spiky face altogether. Sort of heartshaped spiked. But now it's rested. She's lost that hectic look, as if she's about to scratch you with those scrabbly hands. Her eyes are not so much blue as purple. He's never seen eyes that colour. He's heard all about her from the others, of course. Fifteen years old. A kleptomaniac. Bit dramatic that he thinks, but the stories all grow in the telling. He wonders what his own story is, the latest variation. Finds, suddenly, that he doesn't care what it is. They can say what they like now. It doesn't touch him.

He has a way of making the sounds of O.T. go away. Like a valve, so he can slide them away. Make them come back. Like when you're swimming under water and then come up to the echoes and boomings of the pool. Flattened noises bouncing off your head. So different from the sea and the roof of open sky where sounds can spread. The valve is a useful corrective. He can play it like an instrument. No, it's more as if he's conducting an orchestra. A concerto. Together. Blur of radio at the far end, hammering, talk rising and falling in small waves, clatter in the kitchen, the sliding partition sticking in the middle with a grating sound. Laughter. Voices on the tannoy. Hush and noise. Hush and noise. You can regulate it. Move the valve. Blot out all the other sounds. Now the solo. Now there's just the click and crack of Bev's fingers as she breaks off the green tiles from their sheet. Then you can hear her mind is quiet with itself. Move the valve. A scherzo. Some sort of argument has broken out at the hatch. It must be Sean. It is. David's there and the other charge nurse he doesn't like. Sean's stormed off through the swinging doors. Good. Sean used to worry him. Always trying to pick a fight. Now he leaves him alone.

'You got visitors this afternoon, Julian?'

'Don't think so.'

'I thought your mother came on a Wednesday.'

'Not now she doesn't. She has to change buses twice. I told her not to bother.'

'They both came on Sunday?'

'Yes.'

'And your sister?'

'Yes.'

'I think I saw her.'

'Where?'

'Is she thin with long black hair?'

'Yes.'

'It must've been her. In the car park. Did she bring the baby?'

'Why are you interrogating me?' He doesn't like her voice when it rises and shrills.

'I'm not interrogating you Julian. I'm only asking you. Don't be so bloody sensitive all the time.'

'I'm not being sensitive. I just don't like being cross examined. I thought you'd stopped all that.'

'I'm sorry. Really, Julian. I am. Honest.' She touches his arm softly. 'O.K. now?'

Julian makes tight fists and rubs his eyes. 'Yeah.' He tries for the valve. Can't reach it. Can't find it. Winds the green ribbon. Tighter. Now it's all gone out of line. He feels transparent when Bev looks at him. Sometimes. Now she's not looking. That's wise. She's pushing the tiles into place. Carefully. Her eyes seem quite closed. But they're not. They're like a cat's. He needs to say something normal.

'Your tea's going cold.' Bev wriggles in her chair. Swings back. Folds her hands behind her head.

'We could go into town this afternoon. If we're not having visitors.'

'Perhaps I don't want to go into town.'

'Well, there's nothing else to do, is there? And you feel out of it when everybody else has got visitors.'

'Not everybody else has got visitors.'

'Most of them have. We might as well go into town.' Julian feels sly. A surge of malice. 'Shopping?'

'You mean lifting? I haven't stolen a thing since I've been here. Not a thing.'

'Why?'

'Don't need to steal anything now, do I? I mean, I'm here now, aren't I?'

'Is that good then?'

'What? Being here?'

'Yes.'

'Well, it's better than being at home, anyway. And it's better than being in school. It's got to be.'

Something has changed. He moves the valve. He's tired of just her voice. But the concerto does not come. There's noise. There's hush and noise. In and out. In and out. But it doesn't take Bev's voice away. Or the click and crack of her fingers. There's a fierceness about her. Too much cement. Sloppy. Wipe a lot on the cloth.

'When did you first start going with men Julian?'

Julian winds the green ribbon, It's too tight. He'll have to start again. He begins to unravel it. Slowly. Awkwardly. His hand only fits inside the frame with a squeeze. Like this. Sideways. He bites his lip.

'I asked you a question, Julian.'

'I heard.'

'Well?'

That's better. Slacker now. Wind it more loosely. Makes the bands more even. The green is like the green of new beech leaves. Lemony. Still Bev's brittleness sits in the air. Must deflect it. Needs to. Knows how.

'When did you start to steal?'

Bev laughs. 'Is that important? Do you think that's important?'

'I don't know whether it's important or not. I asked you a question, that's all. Do you want another cup of tea?'

'No.'

'I suppose we might as well go into town.'

'Have you been to the abbey?'

'I didn't know you were religious, Beverley. You never told me.'

'Don't be silly.' She thumps him on the shoulder. 'It's ruined. By the river. There's a sort of park and it's nice there. And we don't have to go anywhere near the shops. That make you feel better?'

He almost laughs. A concession. She *is* different. 'M'mm. Slightly.... I don't want you arrested when you're with me.'

'Show you up?'

'Something like that.'

'Draw attention to you?'

He can't get the ribbon right at all. Bev watches him. Her nose wrinkles. It's the little animal again. Contempt makes him clumsy. An idea.

'Why don't we swap over? You wind the ribbon. I'll fix the tiles."

'No way. This is my job. You don't know the effect I'm trying to get.'

'What's special about it? You're just choosing the green bitty tiles.'

'They 're not green bitty. You do say stupid things, don' t you? This is very subtle arrangement.' She flexes her fingers. 'And I thought you were supposed to be artistic.'

'O.K. Bev. It's a very subtle arrangement. It's the most subtle arrangement I've ever seen.'

'Don't be sarcastic Julian.'

'Am I?'

'Bitch.'

* * * * *

The hospital is on a hill. The town is on another hill. There's a mile to walk in between and you go over a narrow bridge with zigzags in it for pedestrians. Right now it's summer and the stream is just a trickle. Julian remembers how it was back in January. He was admitted in January and it wasn't a stream then. Where there's a reedy field full of Friesians there was a sheet of white water. Light and glare and glitterbirds sailing. They hurt his eyes. Julian is walking fast. He always walks fast. Knows that Bev can't keep up with him.

'This isn't a race Julian. My legs are half the size of yours. For Christ's sake slow down.'

'I can't slow down.'

'Course you can. If you want to.'

'I don't want to.'

'Know something? You're childish.'

'God! Listen to the voice of maturity. My guide and mentor.
Who the hell do you think you are?'
'Aren't you cold without a jacket or anything? Just your shirt?'
'No.'
'D'you think it's going to rain?'
'What if it does? We'll get wet won't we?'
'I always feel cold. I always have.'
'It's not cold today. Anyway, it's a long walk. It'll warm you up.'
'There are other ways of warming yourself up.' Bev hurls herself
at him, grabs him round the waist. Pinches him hard. So it hurts.
She giggles. 'I said they'd be alright, didn't I? They think we're
good for each other.'
'They must be out of their tiny minds.'
Bev starts to laugh. She laughs till she almost chokes and the
tears roll down.
'I like you Julian. I do. I do really. And stop looking at me like
that.'
It's a steep hill that takes you into town. It climbs through
terraced houses of yellow brick. Shiny brick with red patterns
round the windows and in a line under the roof. Window boxes.
Lobellias. Trailing campanulas. Cats sat on doorsteps. Then the
street widens. Opens out. There's a market. Stalls hung with jeans
and kagoules and macrame handbags. Crowds of people. Children crying. Dogs sniffing round litter bins and cocking their legs
in greeting. Charlie's Pantry. Sizzling with smells.
'Don't worry,' says Bev. 'Don't look so nervous. I'm not going
anywhere near the market.' She propels Julian down an alley.Tall
garden walls. Laburnum. Syringa. 'See. This is a short cut. This
way we can get to the river without a shop in sight.'
'Where is this abbey anyway?'
'I told you. You take the path just by the bridge where the trees
are. And you can buy me an ice cream in that Lido place. Coffee
and chocolate chip.'
'I can, can I?'
'Yes. My reward for showing you. And I want to show you a
tree in the grounds.'
'I have seen trees before you know.'

'Not this one. I bet you haven't seen this one. It's a medlar. You're supposed to eat the fruit when it's rotten.'

'How nice.'

The alley joins another. They cross and interweave. A sequence of trades-men's entrances. The backs of town houses with long thin gardens. Merchants' houses. Prosperous late Victorian. Little attic rooms and dormer windows. It's a sleepy hidden part of town. Unexpected. Trust her to find it. They must be getting near the river by now. They keep going downhill. Scent of blossom. Litter of white petals. A wall to the right of them erupts with pigeons.

'You're walking fast again Julian. I can't keep up. Hang on.' She races up to him.'Let me lean on you for a minute. I've got a stone in my shoe.'

Everything is very clear. He sees her small rough hand in close-up, a different roughness against the scratchy texture of the wall. Very clear. Shining.

'D'you know what the very first thing I stole was?'

'No.'

'It was a skirt. From Dorothy Perkins.'

'Who's she?'

'I'll ignore that. It was the wrong length and the wrong colour. I don't think I wanted it at all.'

'D'you want me to ask you the obvious question?'

'Why I stole it?'

'M'mm.'

'I don't know really. If I knew I wouldn't be where I am now, would I?'

'Down a back alley with me?'

'There you go again. Pretending you don't know what people are talking about when you know you do. It's just stupid.'

'Like the way you keep asking questions.'

'That's not fair. I've stopped. When did I last ask you a question? The kind you don't like I mean.' She looks up at him. Her eyes are suddenly sharp and dark. 'Anyway I'm asking you one now, to make up for not asking before. All that control and you didn't even notice. Are you listening?'

'Haven't got much choice, have I?'

'Do you answer the doctors' questions?'

'Enough.'

'Enough to keep them off the scent?'

Julian sighs. He's suddenly tired. Tired of word games and valves in his head that will or won't work. You can never tell. Right now he closes his eyes, lets the sound of far off traffic rock him into a soft, even place far from these cinders, this brickdust. High walls. Like a maze. Paint blistered doors. A blackbird sings a sleepy phrase on a lilac bough. For a moment he doesn't know where he is. What's hit him. Bev's grabbed him, pushing him up against the roughness of the wall. Is she laughing at him? Is she angry?

'I don't believe you're queer at all, d'you know that? Not really queer. That's another game Julian. I'm right aren't I? Why don't you face up to yourself?'

'Me? Me face up to myself? How the hell you've got the nerve.... You can talk about games. You never stop. You're the expert. Sort your own sodding problems out, can't you. Leave mine alone.'

The blackbird, if it is a blackbird, hidden somewhere in a high green froth, warbles again in the emptiness.

'I'm not getting at you, Julian.' She looks down at the ground. making a circle in the dust with her shoe. 'I'm interested, that's all. I'm just curious. An inquisitive mind is a sign of intelligence.'

'Use it then.'

They're walking again. His legs feel heavy. It's these tablets. Must be. Make him feel as if he's disconnected from himself. Kind of short circuit. Power cut. Bev's level with him now. Making a real effort to keep up. He has to smile despite himself. She's so *little*. Really little. She misunderstands the smile. Smiles back at him.

'Hold my hand,' she says.

And he does.

* * * * *

'D'you like it here?'

Julian likes it very much. He doesn't want to go back. He could stay here for ever. He's got a new variation on the valve. Sights and sounds now. He can blur and blend his vision of things. So the gold grey stone of the abbey, all the different greens of the different trees, the water and the light on the water, the ducks, the dappled hanging leaves, all fuse into one whirling pattern. Colour without form. Comfort. Well, there are shapes but they don't have to mean anything. They can come at you one at a time. That's the valve again. Be selective. He slides out the blur and the blend. Zooms in on this, on that. A particular duck. A particular leaf. The railings. Glinting. Through the willows the traffic on the bridge. Blue buses. No one can see them here. Inside the tent of the tree. It's theirs. A tiny spider spins on a thread. Abseils against the trunk. Rough furrowed bark. Swerve. Swivel. Bev's face. Heart-shaped. The colour of those eyes.

'We'll have to go back in a minute. We're supposed to be back by the end of visiting.'

'We're already late.'

'Are we? I haven't got a watch so I'll blame you.'

'Typical,' says Julian. He's lying on the pale thin grass under the tree. It's not a bit cold. Even Bev agrees it's not cold. She's alongside him. She doesn't say much now. There's something different about her. But it's not fierceness. Her scrabbly hands are still. The skin is raw pink. Looks sore. He touches her hands. Very gently.

'Do they hurt?'

'They itch. I try not to scratch them. Makes them bleed.'

'Are they always like this?'

'Worse sometimes. Depends. Horrible aren't they?'

'I don't think they're horrible.'

She looks uncomfortable. Embarrassed. Kindness is rare. How to treat it? How to cope? A plastic bottle in the water near them drags against roots. Makes a glugging sound.

'You didn't mind touching them?'

He shakes his head. To prove he didn't mind he touches them again. Strokes them lightly.

He doesn't want to leave. Just stay like this. Him and Bev. Keep it like this. Sights and sounds. The valve is a useful device. It controls the world. Drone, faint drone of traffic on the bridge. Louder. Softer. Greens blurring, blending. The colour of the ribbon. Lemony. Her uneven teeth. Their slight roughness rasps uneven against his tongue.

* * * * *

The next day it's raining. Heavily. There must be cracks in the guttering around the O.T. building and at one spot the water gushes through, bouncing back up off the concrete. Julian runs from the men's block. Not wearing a jacket. Just a tee shirt. Likes the warm feel of the rain on his arms, on the back of this neck. Blinks through wet lashes. Sees the swimmy nearness of things. The cedar tree is dripping brightly from the tips of its lower branches. A nimbus rings each blue grey cone.

Inside Bev is sat in her usual place. She doesn't look up. She's concentrating. He goes to the hatch for the tea. The ritual of the plastic beakers. There's a lightness inside him like singing. He walks smoothly towards her.

'I don't want tea today.'

'No?'

'No. You can take it away. Give it to Sean if you like. He's sweet and milky like me.'

Joan, the occupational therapist, the older one, is wearing a blouse with a Paisley pattern. Buttons of mother of pearl. The epaulette on David's coat is nearly off. It hangs by three long blue threads.

Julian doesn't take the tea to Sean. He just sets it down on the table. Pulls up a chair. But not near her. Sort of no man's land. Not sat at the table. Not sat away from it either. Sort of hovering. He sips at his tea. Too hot.

Wonders.

'You've nearly finished.'

'I have finished. I was waiting for you.'

Julian looks at her. You can never tell. Her mouth is small and hard.

'Your shade is nowhere near finished. It's supposed to take

much longer to make the base, d'you know that? You'll have to start again anyway. The ribbon's all crooked.'

Julian says nothing. There's something very calm, very fixed about her. Something about her face.

Now she pushes her chair back. Stands there. As if there's a spotlight on her. Picks up the lamp base. Holds it in those sore hands as if it's precious.

'Joan,' she calls. Her voice is large. Like she's an actress. A star. He doesn't know that voice. It's new. It frightens him. 'Look Joan. I've finished it.'

Joan walks over, unwinding wool from a ball. She sees the base is quite finished. It looks good. Green flecked tiles, radiating out from a white tile in the centre. Flowers of a kind. Strong loose daisies.

Bev holds it up for Joan to see. For all to see. Smiles. Very fixed. Pride. Fever.

Then quite deliberately, she drops it. Julian sees it fall. Slow motion. Takes years. Seems to flow. Like water over a cliff. Like a waterfall. Hits the ground in the end though. Smash. Smithereens. A pain in Joan's face. Quick. Like the wind on a pond. Gone as soon as it came. All the hammering stops. The background chatter. The clatter in the kitchen. Hush and noise. Hush only now. A quiet like a hole. He forgets all about the valve. Forgets it exists.

'Get the brush and pan from the cupboard, Julian,' says Joan. 'No, the one by the sink.' She shakes her head at the small fierce shape of Bev. Wants to say something. Doesn't,

Broken glass and tiles. All over the floor. Sharp splinters. He's on his knees. Keeps his head down. Keeps on sweeping with blunt quick stabs of the brush. Keeps on sweeping though there's nothing left to sweep. Doesn't want to look at her. Doesn't want her to see his eyes ask the question. Knows she doesn't know why she did it. Knows that at least. Slowly the talk begins to rise again. Little waves. And all the eyes are on them.

He knows her face is closed. Closed to him. Closed to everyone. He walks across the room to the bin at the far end. Looks out of the window at the rain. Doesn't want to turn. Face her. Face any of them. Sends her thoughts though. Across the room. If she can hear them. If he can reach.

It doesn't matter, Bev. It doesn't matter. Listen. I'm Julian. I'm still here.

Encouraging Vermin

Jo's sleepy voice is a blur in the softness of the room, the smell of clean hair, the faint scent of hot milk and spice.

'Tell us about the rabbit, Nainy.'

'Again? You know that story backwards. You could tell me.'

'No. You tell it. It's better when you tell it.' That's Carol's voice. So much clearer, sharper. I pick up the damp towels, the toys. I stand on the edge of that warm circle. Listening. Waiting. Second time round. I can enter it again, the safety of that childhood ring. If it was safety. If it was there.

'But it's such a sad story really.'

'We like it 'cos it's sad.'

'Do you?'

'Yes.'

And so did I. Why, I wonder? What is the sense of reassurance in a sad story? Repeated of course. Made somehow secure by the knowledge of how it ends. Unlike life. Unlike that story.

'Well, long ago, when I was a little girl just like you two are now, I had a rabbit called Napoleon....'

'No,' says Jo. 'Not there. That's not where it starts.'

'No,' says Carol crossly. 'You're not telling it properly.'

'No?'

Impatience curls her voice. 'You know quite well, Nainy. You start with Captain Roberts.'

'Right. I'll try to tell it properly this time. A long time ago, when I was a little girl just like you two are now, I had a friend called Captain Roberts. He was a retired sea captain and he lived in a little house between the railway line and a big pond where there were swans and a heron and some coots and dabchicks. He was very kind to me and when he saw how wet I used to get delivering the papers, and I used to deliver the papers morning *and* night, Liverpool Daily Posts in the morning and Liverpool Echoes at night, he gave me his big shiny oilcloth cape....'

'But it was too big....'

'Yes it was, so he got Miss Pugh to cut it down to size. It was *still* too big really but it was better than before and it *did* keep me dry. It had kept Captain Roberts dry even in the middle of storms at sea so it was a very strong, very waterproof oil cloth cape....'

'You haven't said about Miss Pugh.'

'You want that as well?'

'Course we do.'

'Especially when it's already past your bed-time?'

Jo giggles winningly, the charming one. Carol looks stern.

'When I was a little girl I didn't have a mummy and a daddy like you. My mummy died when I was born and I hardly ever saw my daddy and my brothers and sisters because they lived far away. But I had to live somewhere, so I lived with Miss Pugh.'

'And she was HORRIBLE.'

'She was very strict because people were very strict in those days and she was very poor, so looking after me meant she had to buy extra food for me, and clothes for me, so that was why....'

Was it mother? I know this is a story for children but have you forgotten? The years it took, the pain, the breakdown after my father died, when the truth came out.... Somehow, you had to face it. And it's all been rewritten again, hasn't it? Whatever the truth is, whichever the version, your face wears the old mask. Why, mother? How?

'Anyway, one day I'd just come back from school. It was winter so it was already quite dark. I came into the shop the back way and there....'

'You haven't said it was called a café but wasn't.'

'Oh no, I haven't, have I? You tell me about that then.'

'Well, it had been a café long ago, and then it was called Oxford Café, but now it wasn't 'cos it sold newspapers and sweets and things but it was still called Oxford Café.'

'That's right. Where were we? I know. I came in the back way down the alley which was all cinders and brick dust and *huge* puddles so you had to tiptoe round the edges or get your feet wet, and I opened the door into the yard. The lamp was lit in the kitchen (there was no electricity in *our* house though there was in some places, like the vicarage and the Dunstey's) and I saw Captain Roberts was there. I was very glad because Miss Pugh never shouted at me when he was there.

'And there, on the flagstones by the door was a big box thing, a crate, with something very white moving in it. The yard was in shadow so I couldn't see what it was....'

'It was Napoleon,' said Jo with unfeigned glee. Carol was cross.

'Let Nainy tell it,' she reprimanded. There is something of the schoolma'am in Carol.

'I was so excited. I ran in and there was Captain Roberts with a big beam all over his face and Miss Pugh looking *rather* annoyed but she couldn't do anything about it because she didn't want to look mean in front of Captain Roberts and it was really very kind of him to bring me a rabbit, wasn't it?'

'You haven't said how he got it.'

'No. He knew a man who bred rabbits and showed them and this one was beautiful, but, because it was born with a loppy ear it would never win prizes so....'

'You had it.'

'Yes. This was my very own white rabbit. We did have cats, lots of them, but they were working cats, not pets, and sort of half wild in a way because they had to fend for themselves and keep down the rats. And there were lots of rats. Big ones. And fierce ones. Because, next door to us on one side was the butcher's shop, and just a bit further down towards the river, the slaughterhouse, and on the other side there was a fruit and vegetable warehouse. That meant there was a lot of waste, a lot of rubbish, bits and scraps the rats could eat, so they were a big problem. And that's why Miss Pugh always had cats.

'Well, I don't think Miss Pugh wanted me to have the rabbit at all, and I'm sure that if Captain Roberts had asked her first she would have said no, just like that, but he'd turned up with it, hadn't he, with the rabbit in its own hutch. And he'd already asked at the warehouse if I could have their leftovers, carrot heads and cabbage leaves and things, for the rabbit to eat, so it wasn't as if Miss Pugh would have to pay for the rabbit's food at all. It wouldn't cost her a penny.

And in the summer I'd be able to pick green stuff for it. Fresh groundsel and chickweed and dandelions. Anyway, it was Captain Roberts gave the rabbit its name. Napoleon. A very grand name for a very grand rabbit.'

'And you loved that rabbit.'

'Yes Jo, I did. Very much. I'd never had anything that was really mine before. And I was able to love it and look after it. I used to come home from school and talk to it, and I was sure it could understand every word I said.'

'Then the rat happened.'

'You're doing it again,' said Carol fiercely. 'Let Nainy tell the story. You're spoiling it.'

'It's alright Carol.' As always my mother's voice was gentle, patient. Why did it irritate me, even over something as slight as this? Why did I find her tolerance so cloying, so false? When I knew it was not false.

'Well, I've already told you about the rats. But I'm jumping ahead and I mustn't. Two and a half years went by. This was the third summer since Napoleon had arrived and a very beautiful, very hot summer it was. And it was special because I'd heard that I'd got a scholarship to go to the Grammar School. Miss Pugh was very proud of me and told everyone about it when they came into the shop so I was happier than I'd ever been in my life.

'Then I saw something quite remarkable. One morning I was coming back into the yard after delivering the morning papers when I saw something in Napoleon's hutch. It was a rat. It was sitting alongside Napoleon, bold as brass, nibbling away at a carrot and some green stuff I'd picked from the bank by the church the night before. I nearly screamed. I was terrified of rats. Miss Pugh had told me terrible things about how a baby's face had been chewed away by a rat, how they spread diseases, and how they'd corner you and attack you if they got half a chance. Anyway, there I was, and there was this filthy dangerous cunning animal sat alongside my Napoleon in his hutch, when suddenly I realised something. Napoleon didn't look in the least bit bothered. They were sitting next to each other as if they were the best of friends.'

'And they were.' For once Carol had cut across the story. Jo looked up, ready to say something, but couldn't be bothered. She was too sleepy, too comfortable.

'That's right. They were the very best of friends. And when I'd got over my shock I had to get over being jealous too. Because I was jealous. I'd always thought Napoleon was *my* special friend. I didn't want to share him with anybody. And certainly not with a RAT!'

Both girls sat up straight now, one on each side of their grandmother. And I saw myself in that same state. A child again. Alert. Expectant.

'Slowly I got used to the idea of the rat. He wasn't always there, of course. He was Napoleon's visitor. It was just as if Napoleon invited him for tea. And dinner. And supper. But the rest of the time he was just an ordinary rat like all the others. He even got a bit tame with me. I'd push some leaves through the netting and he'd nibble at them just like Napoleon. I felt I was very brave, making friends with a rat like that. And I found out how he got in. There was a little hole at the back of the hutch, half hidden under the straw. I decided I wouldn't tell anyone about the rat. And definitely not Miss Pugh. She didn't really like Napoleon, and she would have hated his friend. So I kept it my secret.

'Well, summer went by and soon it was time for me to start at the Grammar School. It was very different. I was the only girl who passed the Scholarship that year and it was strange and lonely for me, going all that way on the bus to that huge new school. The first thing I did when I got home was go to see Napoleon. Sometimes the rat was there. Sometimes not. But then it seemed he wasn't visiting anymore. And I didn't notice what was happening to Napoleon. I should have noticed, but there were so many new and strange people and things in my life perhaps I wasn't paying enough attention. I did notice that Napoleon seemed to have lost his appetite. He would just peck at the stuff I brought him. I think now he was hardly eating at all. He was just pulling and tugging at the leaves and grass but not eating properly. Then one Saturday morning I came back after doing my paper round and there he was lying quite still on the floor of the hutch.'

'And he was dead,' said Jo, her voice dark and sombre. Carol glared at her.

'Yes. Poor Napoleon was dead. And I was heart-broken. He hadn't appeared to be ill at all. Just not very interested in his food. I didn't go in the house to tell Miss Pugh. I knew she wouldn't care or understand. I opened the door of the hutch and pulled him out. He was a big heavy rabbit but he'd never been heavy like this before. I just sat there in the yard with Napoleon in my arms. It seemed like hours went by. Then I noticed something was different. The back of it.

'The straw had been pulled away when I moved him and now I could see that someone had nailed a piece of wood in place to seal up the rat's way in. Then I knew what had happened. Napoleon had pined for his friend who couldn't visit him anymore. And he'd starved himself to death. Miss Pugh must have seen the rat one day. She must have decided it wasn't going to share Napoleon's food. She would have called that "encouraging vermin". But I don't think she knew what she'd done. And anyway there was no point telling her. That would be like criticising and I never dared criticise Miss Pugh.'

No mother. Never. And you never dared criticise your husband either. You found yourself another bully. Unerringly. As if to be tyrannised was natural. Inevitable. Has it ever occurred to you that meant I was tyrannised too? Do you know how long it's taken me to learn anger? The language of fighting back. You managed, after your breakdown, when father died and you had to adjust to life without tyranny, to paper over the cracks. But is that all you did? It cost you. It hurt you. But did it teach you anything in the end? Did it change you?

Something is different. Has the story finished? What's happened? The girls are quiet. Yes, but it's not the same quietness.

Then Carol's up on her feet, running to the door.

'Daddy,' she yells as he lifts her up high in the air. And then Jo's there too, falling over her nightie, tugging at his leg.

'Me, me,' she hollers at him. Laughing, he grabs them both, one on each arm.

'You're supposed to be in bed,' he says. 'What's this, eh?'

This is love. This is safety. And enough to go round. I look at my mother, her face wet with tears the child couldn't cry.

Rabies

I'm glad it's dead,' said Robin, crunching frozen sticks underfoot. 'I hated that dog.'

The first day of the New Year. Ice powder crackling in the lane as Helen and the children slur through piles of beech leaves. Crisp and sharp. On the corner they pass the wolfbear's house, the ivied wall where it used to wait. The ivy creaks in the wind, the tiny sound waiting for the roar. There would be no roar. The wolfbear was dead now.

Helen looked uncomfortable. Hatred worried her, Robin's most of all, though she had to admit the wolfbear was an animal even its owners had been hard put to defend. It looked made up somehow. Invented, like a film monster. A walking catalogue of ferocious breeds.

Clare had run on ahead, hoping, Helen supposed, to see the long-tailed tits on the edge of the plantation. The noise Robin made would frighten everything for miles so if you wanted to see squirrels or rabbits or those big cygnets on the Bishop's Pool you had to sneak out without him, which wasn't easy, or run on in front, which was a bit pointless really because you frightened them away yourself then, didn't you?

'Oh no,' said Robin. 'Look who's coming. Rabies.'

'Don't call her that, Robin,' said Helen. 'It's cruel.'

The sight of the unfortunate Roberta was all Helen needed to orchestrate every instrument in her bleeding heart ensemble. Helen had championed the poor child some months ago when she'd been accused of pouring glue all over Mr Bellamy's model on Open Night. No, Helen could not say who had done the dreadful deed but it couldn't have been Roberta. Definitely not. She'd been helping with the teas in the kitchen at the time. Her alibi intact, teachers and committee members had reluctantly let the matter drop. Helen had felt good about it.

Bleeding heart or no though, she did sometimes resent the way Roberta had adopted them all so avidly. Here she was again, moving in on them with her customary lumbering gait wearing as ever those too-tight wellington boots that made a red ridge on her legs. At least the child appears to have good circulation, Helen thought, remembering, wincingly, the chilblained feet of her childhood.

'Did you have a nice Christmas, Mrs Locke?' asked Roberta.

'Yes thankyou,' said Helen, rather stiffly, sensing Robin's cold fury as he stomped alongside her.

'What did you get for Christmas, Robin?'

'Stuff,' said Robin. Hands in pockets. Head down.

'I got a stun gun,' said Roberta, 'and an ironing board.'

Helen felt her mouth twitch.

'Where's Clare?' asked Roberta, positively skipping beside them now, if skipping is possible in wellington boots several sizes too small.

'She's run on ahead,' said Helen faintly, her heart somehow failing to bleed. Robin, it seemed, had had enough of this. He'd always possessed a quite remarkable capacity for acceleration from cold and to prove it he disappeared, literally, in a flurry of beech leaves and a bobbing hood.

'Did he want to go to the toilet?' asked Roberta.

'I don't know,' said Helen.

They were now approaching the kissing gate, a temperamental structure in cast iron. Helen disliked it intensely. It evoked too many memories of embarrassing moments trapped in its maws. There was no sign of Clare.

'Where d'you think she's gone?' asked Roberta.

Helen did not reply. She looked around her at the dark fringe of trees to the right and the bumpy field ahead of them, culminating in the castle mound. It sparkled with hoar frost on its sheltered side.

'Shall I go and look for her, Mrs Locke?' asked Roberta.

'If you like,' said Helen.

She sighed. Although she no longer made a New Year Resolution, this had seemed such a good idea. Simply to step out into a pristine world, to walk off all that food, to ease some of that almost palpable tension Robin and Clare invariably generated when cooped up for too long, and most important, to let Terry nurse his hangover.

She'd cherished an illusion too. That it would be fun. Just her and the children. An adventure. Each tree etched in ice, each puddle glittering. She'd seen how it could be, but it was silly, really, to think it could work. Robin had been sulking ever since the batteries had run down in his Space Invader and Robin's sulks were like his father's. Closed and deep and always threatening more. He'd made his aversion to Roberta quite clear from the start. Clare too, but more mutedly. Helen knew she'd transgressed. Children had such definite views as to how their mothers should behave. It could be very inhibiting.

Now, as the cold minutes creaked past and as she stood there, waiting, watching, Helen had to accept that the adventure was over before it had begun. Clare had obviously slipped off home, sneaking back through the plantation and down the path by the church. Something like a bubble of rage wanted to burst in Helen. She'd worked so hard to make this Christmas good. And it had been awful. She wanted to do something wild. Something crazy. Run out into that crisp clean picture of sky and hill and field, arms flailing. She wanted to yell at the top of her voice, run headlong down that sloping bank where kids sledged when it snowed. She wanted to throw stones.

Her greatest fan beamed up at her. 'We might as well go back now, hadn't we, Mrs Locke?' Roberta's smile, ingratiating, inclusive, envisaged a beaker of hot blackcurrant, a plate of mincepies.

* * * * *

As Helen and Roberta came in sight of the last bungalow in the quiet cul-de-sac known as Abbey Drive, confirmation that Robin and Clare had arrived back before them was provided by the sound of raised voices and yes, breaking glass.

Why didn't the blasted child go home? Fumbling in her various pockets Helen finally produced the key and then, just as she was about to turn it in the lock, the door opened. There was Terry, unshaven, face ablaze, attired in his towelling bath robe which did even less for him now it had shrunk in the wash.

'Where the fucking hell have you been?'

'I think you'd better go home now, Roberta,' said Helen as she stepped inside.

One good thing did apparently result from the fiasco of New Year's morning. There were no more visits from Roberta. Robin and Clare were united in approval and relief.

'Don't ever go talking to that Rabies again,' said Robin.

'Please don't, Mum,' said Clare. Helen was not a political animal. She didn't understand. Identification with victims, she told herself. That's what it is. I must stop doing it. In her mind though, they were still there. The pictures. Pictures of how things ought to be. Should be. More real to Helen than reality. More sharp. More clear. In an attempt to get rid of them she stood at the sink, staring woodenly at the gingham curtains, the stabbing gleam of taps in sunlight. They wouldn't go away. Where did they come from anyway? Those worlds of hers. Worlds where wolfbears were gentled. Worlds where P.T.A. mothers no longer needed to sprinkle their meetings with malice and cold eyes, where teachers believed in fair play. Fair play? Where children loved parents and parents loved children. Simply. Straightforwardly. Where husbands loved wives.

Had she always moved so gingerly round the edge of her life? Had she always been afraid? She didn't know what it was that frightened her but that didn't make it any better. It made it worse. What had the doctor said? Free floating anxiety. It felt *specific*. It hurt. Here in her side. Here like a numb pain behind her eyes. It hurt all the time. First thing in the morning she felt it. Like a taste in her mouth. That jolt. Like a bucket wrenched up from a well. Jagged. Thumping against the walls on the way up. CLANG! That realisation. That this was her life. That Terry was her husband. That her children were her children. That, somehow, as if she'd been asleep for years and suddenly woken, they were just *there*. Claiming. Demanding. Every ounce of her. And she gave all the time. And tried to give gladly. But if only she could have some sense of belonging to them. Not just the other way round. That she mattered to *them*. Was more than just their needs catered for. Made flesh.

She thought of Terry, the way he could, did, in his sleep almost, climb into her body as if it wasn't hers, as if she wasn't there. As a person. Without a by your leave. She was a habit. Something he did. If, in their sleepy tossing, choppy boats on a sea, his mouth brushed against her skin, he would pull her round to him, find what, awake, he called her relevant bits, plunge in as if he was diving. From a great height. That's what she was. A swimming pool. People bobbing about and splashing inside her. Sometimes, in his diving, he was so definite, she vanished right into herself and came out on the other side. And then she knew she was here. That her existence was real after all. That this was *it*. Lying listening to the morning birds, looking at the faint red digits on the clock radio.

The nights were always the worst. The nights of not sleeping. Her mind reeling. Her body heavy as lead. She moved her legs into the quiet coolness. It was a wonder he didn't burn a hole right through the mattress, the furnace that was Terry. She lay quietly, asking herself questions. Why her children were like foreigners. Like things from Outer Space. Why a child like Roberta could be called Rabies, singled out for everyone's contempt, as if it were ordained. Why the world grew more jagged and dark all the time when the earth was still what it had always been. Outside she knew crocuses were pushing up through brown crumbly soil. If she closed her eyes she could feel the corms shift. Split.

Two images kept blurring into each other. Roberta's pained, sly face. And the model. Mr Bellamy's space station, splendid in each tiny detail. Precision. And then that splurge of glue, with, superimposed on that, Roberta's face again. Helen jerked. Bit her tongue. Slight salt taste behind her teeth. The child's absence puzzled her. Perhaps she was ill. Perhaps that was why the days slipped into weeks and still there was no sign of the wellington boots and the smile.

＊＊＊＊＊

One damp afternoon in early February, on her way back from the doctor's, Helen just happened to take the short cut over the playing fields. Some small children in bright hooded suits were playing on the swings. Some mothers Helen thought she knew stood chatting near them. It was then she noticed a solitary figure on top of the slide. It wore a coat that was much too long and a weird knitted hat like a tea cosy. Ought to be in school, Helen told herself, discreetly averting her gaze.

It was too late.

A familiar voice reverberated in the quiet green place. Familiar, yet different.

'My mum says she won't let me come to your house anymore, Mrs Locke,' said the voice, monstrously loud, monstrously accusatory. 'My mum won't let me go anywhere where people use F words.' Then, more quietly, with a kind of soft relish, 'Thought I'd better tell you.'

'Thankyou, Roberta,' Helen mouthed silently, looking up at the bizarre shape in its cage at the top of the slide.

Don't Look

It was *skin*.

And that should have warned me. As she bent down among the washed up sticks and branches her torn coat flapped open under her arm and I saw.

It was wrinkled. It was a peculiar pale grey brown colour and it didn't look like any skin I'd ever seen. It was all in folds. Like a rhinoceros. I bit my tongue and it hurt. The Cae Berllan girls were with me and we were in a good place. She couldn't see us in the spiky bushes on top of Patterson's wall but she could hear us laughing. She kept looking up and scowling. Then she made a fist and swung it round. She was shouting something.

It was November and it was her bare skin under that coat. But it wasn't cold. Not that day. I remember because at the foot of the wall some of the flies that were buzzing about in the ivy flowers had fallen down dead drunk. They were like big bluebottles but green and shiny like tinfoil. They were on their backs and their legs were writhing about in the air.

* * * * *

'They should leave her alone, poor dab.'

Louie nodded. In the sunny window that smelt of hot dust and geraniums they stood and watched Miss Schreider dragging her old tin pram, higgledy piggledy with poking driftwood, the boys behind her at a prudent distance scraping their feet like bullocks at a gate. They were revving up.

'Yer wicked,' they started. Then, louder all the time. 'Yer wicked. Yer a wicked old witch.'

Arnie Edwards was the skinniest boy I knew. He was the leader.

108

There were seven of them. Louie counted them out. Arnie and the Williams twins, his henchmen, then four hangers-on. As they drew level with the tallest geranium on the sill Annie banged her tight fist on the pane.

'That'll do,' she screamed. 'Clear off, the lot of you.'

The four stragglers looked up, ready to run. Arnie and the twins turned and stared, their eyes hard as currants. At that moment Miss Schreider disappeared up the entry in a squeal of pram wheels.

Louie moved from the window. I saw a rush of deep pink climb her neck like prickly heat. She was not in the least like Annie who was the firecest person I knew, and not just with the boys who baited Miss Schreider. Even then I knew, somehow, that she enjoyed her fierceness, that she and Arnie were two of a kind.

Annie...Arnie, Arnie...Annie. I wrote their names in my jottings book. Only the tiniest stroke of my pen separated them. They were almost the same!

Some people said I was priggish. That was not true. My sins were too well documented for me to take any pride in my virtues. I walked a tight line between fears.

'Have you finished your homework?' came the soft voice. Louie fluttered her pale broad hands.

'Yes,' I said. I closed my composition book and put it in my satchel. 'Can I have the button box now?'

'*May* I have the button box *please*,' said Annie, still standing at the window, daring Arnie and Co. to reappear.

Once I supplied the passwords the button box was produced. I started to arrange them all in rows on the heavy tablecloth, the big grey calico covered shirt and pyjama buttons, the jet studs, the brass blazer buttons with the castles, the lions and the unicorns, and my favourites, the delicate painted wooden ones with what looked like tiny pineapples carved on them. By the time I'd set them all out my father'd pulled up outside. I scooped all the priceless jewels back in the box, gave Annie and Louie the ritual kiss and went out to the car. It was round and black and smelt of hot dust again, but not the same as the hot dust in the window. I remember that car like a person. A Standard Ten. My father kept it for nineteen years.

Miss Schreider fascinated me. I didn't know whether to be afraid of her or sorry for her. Perhaps, secretly, like everyone else, I envied her. She could do what she liked. Plagued she might be by the children, shunned by her neighbours, though strictly speaking she didn't have any, reigning supreme as she did in the relics of Quirle Square where all the other houses were boarded up, she could get away with things no-one else dared do. No other woman, certainly, could go on her own for long walks the way she did, turning up anywhere in her torn brown coat and her boots. A picnic at Bonnet's Mill would find Miss Schreider popping up among the sickly scented elderflowers, watching us. A stroll along the Cob with Miss Patterson and her King Charles spaniel, Dandy, would reveal the dark heap of Miss Schreider asleep on the floor of an old boat tied up on the bank.

In Coronation Year, when I was five, we children were all lined up in the High Street to see the Queen drive through. Miss Schreider staged her own welcoming committee on the bridge. As the Royal car glided by she'd shamelessly given a Nazi salute, and from then on, elevated by scandal, she lost some of her shambling gait and seemed to grow taller by a good two inches. Notoriety lent her mythic dimensions. Didn't she have thirteen cats and didn't her house stink to high heaven?

Friday evenings were Annie and Louie's. Always. My mother didn't get back from Babell till late, after visiting my Nain and my Aunty Dilys, who, despite being blind and at least half deaf knew just about everything about everybody. After school I went straight to the tall house in Cross Street and waited there till my father picked me up on his way home from work.

Inevitably, as the years passed, I became less biddable, more questioning. I found myself growing restless in those steep, changeless rooms, increasingly irked by Annie's strictness, increasingly irritated by Louie's placatory manoeuvres. The pleasures of the button box had long since palled. One day, in an attempt to avert another clash between my rumbling pre-pubescent rebelliousness and Annie's dogmatism, Louie sent me to collect a pair of shoes she'd had soled and heeled at Askey's. As the panelled street door opened I was dipped in sharp air.

There was a wind blowing up from the river, the kind of wind that made the ponies dance at Esgair Gwyn. I thought I'd go the long way round to make the most of this, so I turned down the little street that was still called the Fish Quay. It was high tide. The water made a wide mirror curling up at the edges, lapping against the far wall by the laundry with a leafy sound.

By the bridge I saw a familiar shape. It was Arnie Edwards. Fishing. With rare daring I walked up to him, swinging the raffia bag with the red flowers sewn on it, that Louie had given me for the shoes.

'Caught anything?' I asked.

He looked up at me, his thin face blank. I should've known the boy who'd been sent home from school for wearing a Davy Crockett hat in Assembly would never condescend to show the slightest hint of surprise.

'Not yet I haven't.'

'Do you ever catch anything?'

'Course I do. But not here much. It's not much good here.'

'Why d'you fish here then?'

'Because it's nearest.'

There was a long empty pause. 'My aunty sent me on an errand,' I said at last, feebly, annoyed with myself for feeling I had to account for my presence.

'You always go there on a Friday?'

I nodded.

'What for?'

I was trying to think fast. You had to think fast with Arnie Edwards. I couldn't tell him the truth. That I went there because my parents didn't think I was big enough to go back to an empty house.

'Don't know,' I said, conceding defeat. 'Because I want to, I suppose.'

'D'you like them?'

'They're all right. But there's nothing to do there.'

'I think your Annie's an old cow.'

I pretended not to be shocked. 'M'mm,' I said mysteriously. He just sat there, flicking his bony wrist. He had arms like sticks and very long fingers.

'Bet I know something you don't.'

'What?'

'About Miss Schreider.'

'What about her?'

'Bet you don't know she smokes a pipe.'

'Don't be stupid,' I said, getting into my stride. 'It's only men smoke pipes.'

'She does. I seen her. D'you want to see her?'

'Now?'

'Yep. I know where she is. You coming?'

Clutching his homemade rod Arnie advanced with an expeditionary air to the stile that led on to the Cob. I'd never been on the Cob on my own. It was safe enough with Dandy and Miss Patterson, or with the girls from Cae Berllan. But to walk there by myself, worse, to walk there with Arnie Edwards? But there was something in the air. Must've been. A freshness. A leaping. Did I feel any sense of doom? Did I know this escapade would herald a whole sequence of illicit adventures, gathering momentum as they rolled? I don't think so, but here, unmistakably, came my fall from grace.

A cormorant flew up the river, dark and low over the water, and there were gulls circling the poplars up by the piggery. The sky was all around us, huge and tender and high. You were very close to the sky on the Cob. It was like walking into a world of cloud with just the little quaking grasses at your feet to remind you that you weren't flying.

It seemed I'd followed Arnie for hours and still the sandy path snaked out of sight.

'Are you sure you know where she is?' I asked. There was no reply. I'd been swinging the bag expansively to hide my nervousness and the rough threads of the raffia handle had rubbed my palm raw. How long would this take? I couldn't back out now, but what was the time? What if I didn't get back before my father arrived?

'Right,' said Arnie suddenly, in a choked way between his teeth.

'Look down there.'

'What am I supposed to see? I can't see anything.'

He hissed contemptuously. 'D'you see them bushes?'

I screwed up my eyes against the glare. 'Yes.'

'Well, what's by them bushes?'

Then I saw the handles of Miss Schreider's pram, a hundred yards or so down the bank where the river had carved a bay for itself. The high water level had made a kind of lagoon. There were brambles, a grey wedge of sand and two thin alder trees entwined together. I envied her that place. Silently, stealthily, we crept through the grass on our hands and knees. Then came the voice.

'I was wondering when you'd arrive.'

Where had it come from? Whose could it be? It was rich and deep and what Miss Price in Standard Four would describe as nicely modulated. It was a cultured voice, the voice of a lady and an English lady at that. There wasn't so much as a trace of donner and blitzen any where near it. It couldn't possibly belong to Miss Schreider.

There she was though, and quite at home. She was sunning herself in a sandy hollow, a splendidly twisty collection of driftwood piled beside her. She'd kicked off her boots and her feet were bare. And filthy. I looked away, thinking she wouldn't want anyone to see her feet in that condition, forgetting, for a moment, that this was The Outlaw, for whom everyday, normal considerations just didn't apply.

Then I realised something had happened to Arnie. He seemed to have collapsed at my feet and was making the strangest noises. Was he ill? Was he laughing? I couldn't tell, but he was lying there all right, looking most peculiar, wriggling about and biting his arm. I saw the teeth marks on it afterwards.

'Oh God,' he managed to burst out at last. 'Oh Jesus. Look. No, don't look. She's not wearing KNICKERS!'

I looked. He was quite right. She wasn't.

* * * * *

I don't know what happened to Miss Schreider when Quirle

Square was demolished. All I do know is that the village never saw her again and wherever she went her thirteen cats went with her. I don't know what happened to Arnie Edwards either. In the end. Strangely, he didn't tell his gang about what happened that day. Or didn't seem to. We never spoke to each other again.

Today I went back for the first time in more years than I care to remember. Louie, the last of the line, had died, three days before her eighty-ninth birthday. It's true I felt guilty for never going to see her. I'd send cards at Christmas, little presents from time to time, scarves and handkerchieves, that sort of thing, but I couldn't bring myself to go back. The person I'd finally made of myself couldn't breathe in that air

A cold east wind was blowing up the river, so why did the memories of summer stay so clear: hot dust, the path on the Cob, the smell of geraniums? Summer and Annie. Her stiffness, her stillness. Forever stationed in her stifling window, coiled in her knot of frustration and rage, trying so hard to fit herself and everyone else into an invisible box.

Respectability. Decency. The Way to Behave.

The Eye of the Cyclamen

On the table there is one pink flower. It must have fallen while she was out. Now it lies there like some strange marine creature washed up on the shore. She lifts it cautiously as if it might bite. Six petals radiating starlike from a purple centre, and underneath it a cream gold powdering of pollen.

'That you Hilary?' Her mother stirs in her chair. Hilary turns and smiles, holds the flower up for her to see.

'Looks like a starfish, doesn't it? Or an octopus with six legs.'

'Arms, dear. An octopus has arms.'

Hilary says nothing. Arms, legs, what does it matter? It has eight of them, whatever they are, and I was only trying to make conversation. The kind you like to hear. The kind that doesn't mean anything.

'Had a nice snooze?'

'I wasn't asleep, dear. Just having a little think.'

But of course.

'Cup of tea, mother?'

'That would be nice, Hilary. Is it still raining?'

She leaves that question unanswered, scoops up the single bloom and carries it through to the kitchen. Sets it on top of the bread bin where it watches her as she fills the kettle. A sinister pink eye, but it's not sinister and it's not an eye, that's just a game I'm playing, and it's not an octopus or a starfish. And anyway I can't be bothered.

Hilary leans against the sink, half sways, closes her eyes.

I wonder how long it will be before she actually asks me what happened today. And that's another game I'm tired of playing. Timing the responses. And the non-responses. I'm too old for this kind of thing, these neurotic defences. And yet they *are* defences, aren't they? The kind Simon hasn't got.

A tray and a traycloth. Not ironed, admittedly, and more than a little dingy with a coffee stain on it. But I can hide that under the plate. The overall effect is dainty, ladylike. The china is pretty. The cup chimes sweetly against the saucer. The biscuits are decorous, fluted round the rim. Coconut, her favourite. We aim to please. It's getting dark early tonight. I'll pull the curtains, block out the grey and the damp. It's more like November than March. And yesterday was Mother's Day. The cyclamen stands in pride of place. The card. But this year I didn't fix it for Simon to send her one, did I? For Grandmother on Mother's Day. I couldn't manoeuvre that particular hypocrisy, Simon. Criminal damage and actual bodily harm.

And the cyclamen starfish winks as she carries the tray through to the sitting room, to the quiet fire, the gentle clock.

* * * * *

'Early to bed for me, I think.'

'It's only ten to ten, mother.'

'Yes, but I'm tired tonight. And it's my rota day at the Friendship Club tomorrow. I promised Mrs Mottram I'd help with the flowers so I'll need to be there first thing. Haven't you finished that crossword, Hilary? I don't know where you find the patience. All that tenacity. So like your father.'

'It's a stinker today.'

'Throw me a clue, dear. See if I can rustle something up.'

Hilary bites her pen. Slowly a rare smile seeps.

'O.K.'

She licks her lips.

'How about this? You ready? Thirteen down. Operates this way when maternal evasion rules, possibly.'

Silence. The fire coos softly as the coals slip. And the clock ticks. Louder and louder the clock ticks. Hilary watches under her lashes as her mother's face assumes its coy slant, its charmingly childlike opacity.

'Could it be an anagram, I wonder?'

116

'Possibly.'

'Oh dear, Hilary. Beats me, I'm afraid. The old grey matter can't rustle anything up tonight. Are there any letters to help me?'

'Not yet. No help there. It's been puzzling me for hours.'

Perhaps she can't see my face in this half light. Can't see my wicked grin. What would she do if she did? If she thought I'd made it up? What would she do if I screamed it at her? Shall I? Do I dare? OPERATES THIS WAY WHEN MATERNAL EVASION RULES, POSSIBLY. I don't dare. And it's not worth it. She wouldn't understand the joke. If it is a joke.

'I'm stumped, Hilary. I'll have to give up. Now dear, you won't sit up all night doing that crossword, will you?'

'No mother.'

'You look tired.'

'I'll be off upstairs now. Goodness. I'm so stiff. Too much sitting in the chair today. Lazy me.'

She really is going. She really is. Without saying a word. I can't believe it. But I'm not going to let her off the hook. Not this time, for Christ's sake.

'You haven't asked me about Simon, mother.'

'Well?'

'I didn't like to ask, dear. You looked so upset when you came in.'

'Did I?'

'Well, yes. I thought you did rather.'

'Why didn't you say something then?'

'I thought it best not to, dear. I thought you'd like to forget it.'

'Forget?'

'Yes, I thought, well, poor girl. Poor Hilary. It must be terrible for her going there, seeing Simon in that terrible place. I should hate it.'

'I do hate it.'

'That's what I mean, dear. That's why I didn't say anything. Thought it much the best way. Let her put it behind her, I thought. Let her have a pleasant evening. After that long journey. So tiring. And this awful rain.'

'Yes, the rain was really awful, mother. Goodness. How awful it was. I got really wet. Soaked through. Right down to my undies, mother.'

'There's no need to adopt that attitude Hilary, that tone of voice. That's most unlike you.'

Shock. For a moment. Almost. A fleeting sense of something wrong. But then the smoothness falls on palace walls. Or somewhere. And such smoothness. How does she do it? Mother, I've got to hand it to you. You're in a class of your own.

'I know you're upset, dear. Of course you are. You were just the same when you were so high. I used to tell your father. Hilary *will* bother her head. She *will* keep bothering her head about things that don't matter.'

'Don't matter?'

'Now don't misunderstand me, Hilary. I'm not saying Simon doesn't matter. Of course he matters. But worrying about it won't help, will it? Not now.'

'Some people don't find it that easy to switch off, you know. Some people haven't developed your total immunity.'

'I think that's very unkind, dear. Now, where did I put my glasses?'

* * * * *

It's the cold that wakes her. With a start. The banked fire is a thin glow.

Talk about stiff! I should know about stiff. My neck. God! And it's three o'clock! Why...oh yes. She's amazing. My mother is truly amazing. This crossword, for instance. Same newspaper. Same crossword. All these years and she never answered a question once. Not once! She hadn't got a clue. Literally hadn't got a clue. And it's the same phraseology. Exactly. Grey matter. Rustle something up. And my father never told her not to bother. To stop pretending. They played the same game. The collusion in the illusion game. And she's still doing it. And it still works. She's got herself off the hook again. Didn't ask me about Simon in the end. Didn't want to know. If it's not nice I don't want to know. Her philosophy. It works. For her. How? Because she's made of teak, that's how. Solid mahongany.

Is it her limited vocabulary? Is that the secret? Those acceptable epithets. Nice. Little. Pleasant. And if it's not nice or little or pleasant, or better still all three, it must be silly. Or unkind. Sprinkle them around. Along with ladylike, of course, and pretty. Oh yes, and dainty. Don't forget dainty. But they don't *mean* anything. They do though. Well, terrible does. It means taboo. Simon's in a detention centre. Taboo. Awaiting a psychiatric assessment. Taboo. Social reports. Taboo. And I'm divorced. Taboo. And I shouldn't have married him in the first place, should I? Taboo. And what's worse I'm very unkind I am. I say things. I shall change my name. Hilary Bloody Taboo. That's me. Hyphenated.

I understand you, Simon. I do understand. Perhaps that's the problem. Christ! Right now I wouldn't say no to a spot of criminal damage myself. I'll even go one better on the bodily harm bit. Perhaps I'll find a dash of G.B.H. is good for the soul. But not outside the Kentucky Fried Chicken or wherever it was. No. Here. Right here. Right now.

Sitting in the cooling room, rubbing her aching shoulder, Hilary feels too tired to move, too tired to go to bed. She hates the figurines on the mantlepiece, the Coalport cottages with the roses crawling out of the chimneys. That's where the smoke should be. She hates all the accretions, the layered associations, the twee tastefulness. Back in her childhood home along with thirty nine years of pent up aggression.... If she were to move one muscle surely the whole room would disintegrate. It would have to. It would have no choice.

I haven't got your courage, Simon, your honesty. Your incisiveness. And I haven't got your special talent for self destruct. No, I observe the niceties, don't I? I was nicely brought up. I still follow the rituals. Remember the drill?

If you feel a temper coming
Count to ten:
If that doesn't solve the problem
Count again.

Well, it didn't solve the problem, Simon. It never did. What was the next bit?

Start to count the things around you,
Count the things that you can see.

Right. Here goes.

There are seven flowers on the cyclamen. Seven perfect pink flowers. Now isn't that strange? When they're actually on the plant they don't look a bit like starfish. Or octopusses. Octopussi? Well, whatever they are, they don't. Start again. There are four cushions on the window seat. Good girl, Hilary.

There are three books on top of the piano. There are three crumbs on the traycloth. Three quiet brown crumbs....

Tangled Ewe

B ut you must rest, Laura.'
'I know.'
Oh, how I know.

This house is old. It sags. The lintel bears scratched figures, a small carved pineapple. If you climb to the roof it's like being out at sea, squinting through a porthole. I'm transparent. I'm plotting my course through time. I'm bringing myself back to the beginning. To the birth of the house. The rafters are new again. Their scent is forest trees. All has been planed white smooth. Moist curls. And the roof is open and full for the birds and the clouds.

'Am I getting on your nerves?'

'No. Course not. It's just that I wish things were better for you here. More restful. I mean, hell Laura, what a place for a convalescent!'

'I could hang out the washing.'

'Well, yes, you could, but do you want to?'

I explain that I feel like a spare part. That it will help to be able to do something. And after all I'm not physically ill, am I? Just crazy.

'Don't say that,' says Carly fiercely, handing me the baby's bath full of washing and a plastic bag full of pegs. 'Mind you, the way Martin behaved it wouldn't have surprised me if you really had gone bananas. That man!'

'It wasn't his fault.'

'Come off it Laura. God, I'm not going to be drawn into that again. You know how I feel about him.' She makes one of her expansive sweeping gestures. 'On a practical level, put my wellies on. They're by the back door.'

'I should've brought my own.'

'How were you to know you'd be living in a mud bath?'

How was I to know anything? It was the end of June when Martin got me into the hospital. But all I needed was time. Time to grieve. Wasn't that natural? Dear Dr. Martin Brinkley. Thank you for everything. And now it's November. And Carly has saved me. Not for the first time.

I'm glad to get out. The wind stings my face. I wrestle with it gladly, buffeted, flapped, spun alive.

I pick my way through the rubble at the side of the house, past the caravan. Robert's up on the scaffolding. Tom stands by the concrete mixer, his expression one of intense pride. It's his responsibility, the mixer, and all his ten year old's energy is concentrated on it, its comfortable slooshing sound, its dependable revolutions.

The mud sucks on my boots. How open it is. Hill after hollow, fold upon fold. I climb up the bank to the washing line. A buzzard mews above us, circles, soars, planes. I can't believe I'm here. Free.

I scoop up the washing. Aphra's dungarees. Robert's shirts. Lumberjack check. And Tom's, a smaller version of his father's. Now Cicely's nappies and Babygros. Can I handle it? I must. I have to. I have lost my child. I have lost Jamie. And I'd waited so long. It's so ironic. There's Carly. Having her babies was easy as shelling peas. And me, the doctor's wife? Miscarriage after miscarriage. And then after all the cossetting and dedication, and no one, not even Carly, can deny how dedicated Martin was when I was pregnant, finally, the miracle. The arrival of Jamie. Followed by the black hole. The gaping agony. I can still feel the hollow in the room. *My child is not breathing.* I can still hear the mobile above his cot, the dolphins and porpoises spinning, tinkling, their sweet mocking chime.

Cot death. Cot death.

There madness lies. Come on Laura Brinkley. You've got a job to do. Watch you don't drag these sheets in the mud.

* * * * *

'Are you sure you'll be alright in the house?'

'Yes. Of course I'll be alright. I love the house. Even if it's not all there!'

'God, I'm some sister. Can't even put a proper roof over your head.'

'There may not be a roof but there is a ceiling,' whispers Robert. 'Keep your voice down Carly. You'll wake Cicely again.'

We sit in the cramped caravan kitchen, clutching our mugs. French Onion Soup. With Croutons. This will be the first night for me to be in the house on my own. I've been here for a week now and since I arrived Carly has slept alongside me, both of us in sleeping bags on the floor in the one habitable room.

'There just isn't room for us all in the caravan. It's a hell of a squeeze as it is, so I'll have to deny my poor husband his conjugal rights until you can cope on your own.'

'Conjugal rights?' Robert whistles. 'After I've been up on that roof all day you've got to be joking.'

Carly's so wise, so sensible, still the big sister. She'll help me out but she won't mollycoddle me. Where would I be without her? I know only too well. On those first nights she wanted to be there with me, and I was glad. I was scared of my own shadow. We talked into the early hours, as if we were girls again. It seems so long ago. It seems like yesterday. I thought of Robert in the caravan with the three children, and I thought, oh Carly, how lucky you are. You're so safe. Robert makes you safe. You make the children safe. You spin a web of warmth and work. And it's good work. Tom's a little man already. Aphra with her red hair and that quick temper, she's like you at that age, Carly. And Cicely, I suppose she's more like me.

'That's right,' says Carly. 'She's a hypersensitive little twirp.'

I've finished my soup. 'You sure you'll be O.K?' asks Robert.

'Yes. I've got the torch, and anyway, I feel so safe here. You know what this means to me....'

'Here we go again,' says Carly. 'Now don't start on another paean of praise. We only did what anybody else would have done. We're *family*.' Then more seriously, 'Just wish we'd realised sooner, that's all. Been able to do something right at the start. We had no idea. Why didn't you write to us, tell us? Why didn't that bastard of a husband of yours....'

'Shut up,' says Robert in a stage whisper. 'Stop holding post mortems.' Now that's a remark that would have had me plunging back into my morass only days before. I must be getting better.

* * * * *

There are no curtains on the windows. Well, they'd be super-fluous, wouldn't they, when there's no roof? There's no electricity, no mains water. There is a well. It's in the front garden, in the bank under a rowan tree. It's faced by a thin metal grille.

'To stop dipsomaniac hedgehogs falling in,' says Carly.

The first time I went for water a brilliant ash leaf was spinning in it, like a lemon blade. I watched it. I lost all sense of time. It was a leprechaun boat. I watched it sail. I followed its slight bobbing movement as the spring bubbled under it, kept it buoyant, like a flame. A something sacred.

'Where have you got to?' says Carly, finding me. 'Come on, I need that water. Stop playing vestal virgins or whatever it is. Robert! This woman's worshipping the well for God's sake. This may be wild Wales but they're all respectable chapel people round here, you know. Don't take kindly to pagans!'

You rock me back to reality with your humour, Carly. Your brisk no nonsense.

The fire shifts. It casts a gentle pattern of rose and gold on the wall. The sleeping bag lining tickles my chin. I stretch out, flex my toes. I watch the moon creep in and out of the clouds.

Tomorrow we're going to Aberaeron. Shopping. Carly, me and the girls in the landrover. After Robert's taken Tom down to the village. To school.

* * * * *

Martin had parked his car on the far side of the caravan so I had no warning. Robert semaphored to us from his perch on the chimney, but before the information could sink in the door opened. The scratched figures, the small carved pineapple, that loving homely lintel and beneath it, Martin. His face is closed.

124

I am afraid of this man, Carly. Carly I'm afraid of him.
'How are you, Laura?'
Carly's carrying Cicely. Aphra clutches my hand. Or is it the other way round?
'She's none the better for seeing you,' storms Carly, bringing herself up to her full height. Whatever impact she's trying to make is lost on Martin. Cool. Imperious. Impervious to all her bluster.
Robert has appeared now, wiping his hands on his overalls.
'I'll knock off for a bit. Time for a tea break before I go and fetch Tom. We'll go in the caravan, Martin. No mod cons in the house as yet.'
'Since you're here I suppose you'd better join us,' Carly snarls at Martin, and now in her anxiety, she's pulled Aphra away from me, is dragging the bemused child along behind her. 'You can see how the other half lives.'
How different they are, Robert and Martin. Rob is bear-like, short, stocky, hairy. Martin has lost none of his elegance. His arrogance. Where do I look? There's no avoiding eyes in this cramped interior. Cicely is crying again so I hold her as Carly clatters the tea things. Excessively. Even when I try to look away I still see his towering shape. Or feel it rather. There's mud on his shoes. A little has splashed up on the hem of his trousers. And I've loved him for so long. Am still in awe of him. But now I shrink immediately in his presence. Feel childish. Inadequate. Isn't that what I am?
I remember Carly's words, 'He'll always put you down. It's the way he's made. Don't know what his patients think of him but I think he's a first class bully.'
'He's very good with his patients,' I'd said feebly.
Carly snorted contemptuously.

* * * * *

'Well, he's gone. Thank God. Sound the all clear, Robert.'
Yes. He's gone. But not for good I don't suppose. Can I envisage life without him? Does he really want me back? What for? To start it all over again, the belittling syndrome? The recriminations saga?

I've had enough of your quiet sneers, Martin. Your unspoken contempt. I can do without it.

Can I?

To everyone's surprise I announce that I'm going out. I tell them I want to walk in the hills, let the wind blow the feeling, the fear of Martin away, let my mind uncurl.

I want time and space to think. I want to decide what the future means. What choices I've got.

Robert looks apprehensive. Let her go, Carly's eyes tell him silently. She smiles at me.

Her wisdom holds me as I walk into the lane, its deep ruts, the watery hollows between them spattered with ash keys. It's sheltered here under the steep bank and the hedge. The mud is smirched with what look like yellow marbles. I think they're crab apples.

I climb over a gate on to a high sheep pasture. The tousled ewes eye me nervously, nostrils flaring. They fling and scatter. The further hills are rainlit but here the air is dry and sharp. As I walk the wind lifts me, wraps itself around me.

I'm not really thinking but the wind thinks for me, loosening the strands. It's then I see her, a ewe in the hedge. She's quite alone. As I get near her she bucks. Tries to rear. Is she stuck? She must be. Straining to pull free her coat becomes more entangled still in a braid of bramble and wire. I get closer. I'm not that used to animals but murmuring something I try to soothe her. The fleece on her far side is hooked. I try to hold her steady with one hand as I work with the other. She's afraid. So am I. She panics. Her feet keep sliding on the thin slope. She can smell my fear.

What can I do? Martin's voice is in my head. Just look at you. You're hopeless. You can't do anything. To add insult to injury the ewe pees fiercely, the warm wet a rush on my leg. I want to laugh. I want to cry. Then it's Carly's voice I hear. Thank you very much, you silly bitch. I'm only trying to help and I don't need watering. I look around me. Emptiness. Nothing but grass, hawthorn and sky. Not a farm in sight. I'll make my way back. She'll have to be cut free. Surely Robert will have some wire clippers. Something. I run down the slope now. Not too fast or I'll go flying. I've just reached the first gate and the cattle grid when I see a landrover coming this way. Robert? Of course it isn't. I want to disappear.

Well I can open the gate at least. I can do that, can't I? I do, and as the farmer nears I wave him to stop.

'There's a ewe stuck in the hedge up there.' I point to the spot but the brow of the hill has hidden her.

'Right,' he says. 'You'd better jump in and show me.'

My Friend of the Earth

I'm glad it's March anyway. Means every time someone comes into the hall and knocks the calendar off the hook we don't have to gaze down at a pair of mating dragonflies in glorious technicolour. So why don't I move the calendar? Tradition, I suppose. I've always had a calendar there. By the phone. But this one? So wide and bulky in a hall so small you can't even swing that proverbial feline? Well, Tom gave it me, didn't he? It's a long story.

Recycled paper too. *Mais naturellement.* And why should I squirm? What could be more natural than a splendid pair of insects locked obliviously in coital bliss?

Anyway, it's a tree this time. More photogenic. Tasteful. Lit from below and seen through a pink filter. A Jeffrey pine. Never heard of it. The heart of the tree. A Clapham junction of splayed branches, crusted with ice and a snow powdering. On a rocky dome high above Yosemite. Wow! Funny, isn't it, how someone who can get so worked up about natterjack toads and rare wetland flora can be so, well, cavalier about the feelings of a human, female of the species. Me, for God's sake.

Not that you could class him as a cavalier. More of a roundhead, really. I speak figuratively. Hell, what do I care about Tom?

Sally says I'm suffering from a classic case of Other Woman Syndrome. She should know. She's had her share of that particular malady. But it's Easter, isn't it? School's out. And not a moment too soon. The time of rebirth. Yessir. You have been warned.

I'm going to become a born again sybarite. I've bought myself a very expensive Easter egg. I've never done that before. And I've got myself myself a whole sachet of those gorgeous bath pearls. I was given some for Christmas a while back and I rationed them.

Sunday baths only. And only one at a time. But I intend to make up for that parsimonious restraint. I shall indulge myself shamelessly with a succession of long Easter soaks. *La Peste* can wait. I know I've been pestering Clarkson to let me teach some VIth Form, but right now I need the bubonic plague like a hole in the head.

I shall go into a coccoon for three whole days. And emerge as my new sparkling self. Who am I trying to kid? I shall keep a diary of my transformation. I haven't done any *serious* writing since I can't remember when. Yes I can. In the run-up to the divorce and just after mother died. But that was therapy. This will be Art.

What a pretentious twat you are, Sylvia.

* * * * *

Good Friday. When I was a religious maniac I cried all day on Good Friday. I was four. It had been building up for days and worried my mother sick. I started drawing these pictures of tombs and great stones being rolled away and angels. Anorexic types in the style of El Greco. And I went round the house singing 'There is a Green Hill Far Away' in deep lugubrious tones. We used to laugh about it afterwards. Rather nervously. When I was older and wiser and more robust.

'You were such an earnest child.'

What would you think of Tom, mother? He's earnest too. Quite unlike David, but you did try to like him, didn't you? For my sake. God it makes me want to start snivelling à la four years old. Only I didn't snivel then, did I? When did the snivelling start?

Less of this. I shall go and run my bath.

I could always have a binge on the sloe gin, couldn't I? Memories. Like the colour of your hair. Why do men get in such a state about going bald? Rare wetland flora and going bald. Is there a connection, I ask myself. Doubt it. Yet, just think, right now, in some exceedingly rare wetland an undistinguished seeming plant, the kind you'd need an electron magnifying glass to see, might hold the secret! Alopecia banished from the face of the earth! Perhaps it was there at my feet among the bog asphodel and the spaghnum moss. And I probably trod on it as Tom scanned the horizon for sight of a marsh harrier. In rapt and concentrated mood....

'I don't know why it bothers you,' I said, as the wind whipped his gold and thinning strands, revealing an elegantly bony cranium. 'Anyway,' I said, putting my hand in the clammy pocket of his new waxed cotton coat, his pride and joy, in search of Aniseed Imperials, to which I'm sure I was becoming increasingly addicted, 'Baldness is a sign of virility.'

Oh, the lies we tell....

And the day we picked the sloes.

'I love Wales,' he said, with a proprietorial air that annoyed me intensely. Ah, but do you love me, dear Tom? Your little Welsh French mistress, would you believe, your bit on the side? Where do I stand on the sliding scale of significance in the life of a corporate planner? Where does anyone stand? Sometimes I find myself, yes, I admit it, pining for David's total lack of responsibility, his frivolity, his facetiousness. Earnestness can wear you down. The wife, the kids, the company, the mistress. Don't mistresses get fur coats and flowers and diamonds and expensive perfume? Fat chance. Furs are obviously out of the question with a lover as environmentally sound as Tom. The perfume's not on either, the musk thereof and therein being extracted from the gonads of deer or something. Diamonds are South African. Tom, is your liberal conscience for real? I mean, authentic, like we used to say? Are you just another in a long line of pseuds? Flowers, then? Permissible. At a pinch, perhaps. So why do I think myself lucky if I actually get a birthday card?

Because you're a bloody fool, Sylvia. That's Sally's voice. And tone. Worldly wise. Jaded. Pertinent as ever.

Sloes. All over the hedges above the Elwy. High up among the furze and the bracken, the mewing buzzards, and then suddenly in and out of the hedges, a delectation of long tailed tits, tweeting their almost excruciating high pitched unison cry, their bodies, little pink, white and grey blossoms, those ridiculous tilting tails. And I stand and gulp and grab his arm and see, following them, four or five bullfinches, their breasts like the new deep pink in a child's paintbox, their caps so shiny, so deeply blueblack, with a bloom and a glow on them like the sloes we pick like idiots, packing them tight in a sandwich box, in a carrier bag I have folded in my pocket in case we find an example of that rare wetland specimen. But not up here in the high country. I'm mixing my habitats. See, Tom, what you do to me?

Wherever you are....

Guilt is a terrible thing. It corrodes. And this love, and kid myself as I will, it *is* love, can it be wrong? It doesn't feel wrong and that isn't cooking the emotional books, to justify what I want anyway. I do him good. Of that I am convinced. His marriage is all the better for my occasional ministrations. What harm does it do? And anyway I don't feel guilty. Childhood conditioning and all that and I still don't feel guilty. I just wish we could love and be merry for God's sake. I wish it didn't take me hours to reassure him it *is* O.K. That I'm no threat to the rest of his life. That he's safe. But he knows that.

To be trusted implicitly is to be taken for granted. Yes, Sally, I know that too.

I'm wallowing. It's lovely. And if there are better ways of spending a Good Friday morning I don't know what they are. I think the bathroom is the best room in this flat. It's almost the biggest. And there can't be many bathrooms with stained glass in them. I'm glad they retained that section there above the frosted bit. They knew how to build houses in those days. The Edwardian heyday. And all the little servants' rooms under the roof. What architecture doesn't tell us, eh? About social priorities and social assumptions. The mystique of hierarchies. Know something? I've never understood anything at all. Honest. I've never been switched on to reality. To the abiding truths of Realpolitik. I cling to dreams, don't I? Dare I say I cling to ideals? Why not? Still the little flower power child? And does that mean I never grew up?

Did David grow up? He started grown up, didn't he? Knew how to manipulate, to get his own way. Some might call it charm. Perhaps it was. And though no one could say Tom was *charming* he gets his own way too, doesn't he? Devoted wife. (Well, as far as I know. He never says anything to the contrary.) Devoted mistress. How ridiculous. It's hard to imagine any one as *English* as Tom having anything as continental as a mistress. I'm not a mistress. Well, not in the positive, meaningful sense. Is there one? Not in these exquisitely hypocritical islands there isn't. I'm just an executive toy, ain't I?

M'mm. What's new about this though? I've always known the score. *Plus ça change, plus c'est la meme chose.* Too right. And I can always tell by his voice when he phones, and I'm stood there in my poky little box of a hall, contemplating the mating dragonflies. If he's in one of his bright and bullish modes he's just giving me a quick buzz before zooming off to Adelaide or Islamabad. Milan, perhaps. Kyoto. He's showing off, isn't he? But then, just sometime, just ever so occasionally, the voice is different, isn't it? He needs a little reassurance, bless him. A little ego-massage. Which is where I come in. My God, what a wonderfully convenient little creature I am. I'd like a reassurance station too. Where I could pop in for the occasional service, emerge revived, revalidated. Renewed and rejuvenated.

Tough, Sibs. That ain't for the likes of you.

My feet are a *mess*. The reward of thirty-nine years of neglect. Rough skin. Callouses and prehensile toes! Hideous. Never mind. Tom doesn't notice my feet, does he? I'll ask him next time. Next time? Of course, I don't *know* do I? There may never be a next time. Well, if there isn't it'll be a relief, really. Won't it? Dear Tom, I want to ask your advice about my feet. Perhaps my feet are bugging me the way your baldness (incipient) bugs you. What do you recommend for weary feet, ugly and overused? A long soak, says Tom.

Well, after we'd picked all those sloes we had to do something with them, didn't we, children? So it was back to the flat with a bottle of gin and a recipe culled from an ancient cookery book I found in the library. Hell, I don't even like gin. Mother's ruin, yes? Smells like lavender water....

But somehow, weeks later, that first sip. The sloes so long seeped in sugar, in alcohol, and all the condensed effect of that day in the hills. Not even a soupçon of lavender water, and that rich cloudy purple shade. That fire on the tongue.

Why am I a sentimental idiot? No, don't tell me.

This water's going really cold. Damn, I thought I'd left the immersion on. I meant to. Hell, that's the door bell. Who can that be NOW? I'm not answering. They can go away. And if it's important they can come back. I'm on retreat this weekend. I'm in training for when I become a virtual recluse.

* * * * *

I've always told Tom NOT to land on me out of the blue. And he's never done it before.

Still, there's always a first time, Sally.

You smell nice, he said. I should, I said. Magnolia and lily of the valley bath pearls are very expensive. By the way, I'm glad it's March. I'm sick of looking at those mating dragonflies. Damselflies, he said. Damselfies? I said. Yes, he said. Can't you read? Look. You always were a pedant, I said.

Seasonal Change

The first time it was winter. February. Not cold though, really. She waited till six o'clock. Then all the people would be safe in their tall thin houses. She was afraid of her own transparency. That people could see. Light bulged from cracks in curtains, making bright oblongs on parked cars, on strips of privet. She slipped out quietly. Her mother was watching the News. In her mind's eye she saw deft fingers move over growing knitting, glasses perched low on her nose, lips softly counting.

She saw no one. It was easy. A dog barked somewhere. A cat appeared on a low wall, waiting to be fussed over, stroked, made much of. She gripped the torch in her pocket. She would not need it. An orange glow hummed over the town. As she left the flat streets and edged for the lanes, the farms, darkness did not make the sudden black shape she expected. The sky was a wedge of dark blue with still a pulse of light in it.

Her steps were quick and urgent. Strong. Telegraph poles whizzed by. Seemed to. Astonishing, this speed, this freedom. At the farm they were milking. Bold lights in the yard, the shippon doors held back, the rhythmic machines filling the night, making a focus of huddled roofs and walls. Caravans in the orchard under the great bare shape of the pear tree. Everything pared down to essentials. What did she feel? Exhilaration. Certainty.

Proper country now. A chill in the wind, a hint from the river. Her hands flex in her pockets. She brings out the torch. With deep glee she spins its light into the trees, the sycamore, its broad girth, the symmetry of its branches made spectral, gilded. She finds a child's abandon here, a kind of laughter, a bubble of it, anarchic, fierce, tinged with the joy of extremity. But she is not a child.

Over the first field. The cattle grid. She crosses it, rattling the metal bars. The track climbs steadily. Up there, high on the left, Top Farm in its fringe of poplars, its high gables peeping through twiggy swathes. Something that is neither moon nor starlight bathes the face of the house. No one lives there now, though sometimes, in daytime, it is still alive to the sound of tractors and trailers, collies yelping, boys swinging on gates. The house turns its emptiness, its serenity to the river, the whispering trees. Over the first stile. It's muddy where she lands. Sheep move, soft grey shapes, too sleepy to bleat or warn. She has always had this ability, to move unannounced, unacknowledged among animals, as if accepted, as if part of their life, moving at a different pace, their pace, not part of the hectic life of humans. She walks with glad strides. Extravagant. The grass is longer, wetter. The sky is larger, a basin of deep sliding blue. The murmur of the river fills the air. Over the second stile. Into the lane. More mud. Stickier, then the central section, higher, firm with pebbles.

For centuries this track has led down to the ford, the only place to cross the river before the bridge was built. The first bridge. When was that? Twelfth century? She feels she is part of a pageant. An eighth century saint. A fourteenth century pilgrim. A friar, a Dominican, hooded in black. Soldiers and statesmen. Footpads. Rogues. The folk of the land. The folk blurring and blending. It's as if she hears the thumping of horses' hooves, the slow lumbering of wains, beasts driven to market. Flocks of geese. A dancing bear. Droves of children. She is glad to be saying goodbye.

There were picnics here with her own children. Years back. One more gate, a grey looming stone, the gate post, then the sloped field dips to the right, to a thicket of hazels and thorns. There, where the river makes its broad slow curve, silvery alders grow.

February Fill Dyke. That's what they say but the ground is surprisingly dry. Merely the hint of pulling earth on her shoes. There are cattle in the next field. They low softly. Her presence disturbs nothing. A waterbird, a coot, a moorhen, she can't see, moves unconcerned from the bank with only the faintest clatter. Movements, a chevron shape, on the dark water.

Everything is slowed, is stilled. Her own rage, if that's what it was, her own despair, if that's what it was, where are they now?

She has walked for miles. She feels brightly alive. Tingling. Her skin is tingling. Warm with exertion while a cooling wind skims the river's smoothness. She sits on the bank, hugs her knees. Looks up at the sky's basin. Wonders why she came. Then the rain starts softly, hardly bothering to try.

* * * * *

The best years were the years in the cottage. Easily the best. You lived high in the clouds, literally, on a level with the buzzard, the raven. To your birdtable the green woodpecker came. The jay, shy, elusive, nervous of his raucous cousins, those magpies, those spivs. And in summer your woodwarbler. Creamily slender. Delicate as rain. Drinking in the drenched bloom of the blue flower.

One day a notice in the window of the shop where you bought the wild bird seed:

SIBERIAN HAMSTERS FREE TO GOOD HOME

'Can we have one, mum? Go on, mum. Can we?'

Treetops. That was the name the boys gave her. Inappropriate for a scrap of life that should have known the tundra, treeless, drear. She was fawn grey with a copper undertone, a black streak running down her back.

'They're inbred, you know. Susceptible,' the man told them, lifting lithe shapes from the sawdust.

'What does that mean, mum?'

Treetops was reprieved. Last remnant of a strain bred for research. Out of a laboratory and into their lives.

The boys watched her, busy on her wheel, admired precise feet, eyes burnished like elderberries. Less than three inches of compound energy, she wriggled through two years of their growth. She had her ailments. The allergy that nearly killed her. Dandelion shoots, fresh picked for a spring treat. Acid. Too strong. The abcesses that followed. The antibiotics. The high drama. Absurd really, with lambs clawed by foxes dead yards from their door. She was funny. Cheeky. Frenetic. Loved.

She grew old only gradually but then came the days when she would not eat. She lay in her bedding, huddled, hidden. For the first time she got nasty when they tried to change her water. She would grab for a finger, hang on fiercely, her wheel unturned for weeks.

'She's going to die, isn't she, Mum?'

The boys were matter of fact about it. She's an old hamster.

One day you came down early. Half an hour later and it might have been over. Treetops lay sprawled between her bedding and her water. She appeared to be dead, cold to the touch, but when you lifted her, horror, she sputtered into movement. Back legs paralysed, she heaved her upper body, head squirming blindly.

You knew what you must do. It was the saucepan you used in the power cut. Three days of smoked tea and snowstacks outside. Now blackened and burned, you only used it to steep bread for the birds.

Youl filled it the top with water, walked out into the bird clamouring morning. Scent of lilac, lavender. You gulped deeply then plunged her in, thinking, fool that you were, she would be glad to go. Just mention that word euthanasia. What you see is your hamster's struggle in the saucepan. That last attempt to bite. That final bubble.

* * * * *

The second time it was summer. July. Not hot at all. Wet and grey. This time she waited till half past midnight. Dressed again silently. Wrapped her torch in a plastic carrier bag. Hovered on the landing outside her mother's door. Avoided the creaking floor boards. Softly manoeuvred the stairs.

She saw no one. It was easy. Traffic still hummed far off on the by-pass. Not the long way round this time. She took the road to the bridge, the walk below the church. Still tidal at this point, the river swelled grey green. There was no long preamble. She slipped down from the damp path, step by step, where mud oozed to the brink, leaving the torch in its glistening wrap behind her.

The first shock of the water. Cold. To her bones. Deep. The

current strong. No certainty this time. No energy for that anymore. Simply numbed with a dull pain. Nothing could change now. Nothing could ever be vivid again. Not even this. The water carried her. Her legs splayed loose in the water. Small waves slapped her face. She dipped her head. Held her nose and dipped her head. Again. Again.

This was a big saucepan. There was no help for her. No one would hold her down.

Whistles

Yes, I heard the whistles.

Somewhere on the harbour wall people were blowing whistles. How can you hear sounds so clear, so insistent; how can you tell yourself listen to those whistles and you listen to those whistles and ignore them.

Well, I ignored them.

I swam out blithely. Nine of us swam out in a grey sea. This was 1966. This was Easter Sunday in Spain.

To prove I didn't care that the sea was cold, and it was cold, to prove I was a strong swimmer, and I was a strong swimmer, I swam out the furthest. WATCH ME SWIM OUT THE FURTHEST. It was only when I realised how strong I wasn't, that the currents were stronger by far...that I realised those whistles were warning whistles.

I saw a face today. At a distance. In the next compartment and at the height of the rush-hour, so, I suppose, in all that heaving sea of faces I might have been wrong.

But I wasn't. It was him. Jed. And it might have been yesterday. It was like a little window opened in my head and I suddenly saw what I'd tried so hard not to see. And Jed was my best friend. After adolescence no one ever talks like that, no one ever mentions the term...BEST FRIEND. Let's face it, it's so, well, adolescent.

At a distance. Yes, but somehow in terms of essentials he hadn't changed. Have I? Our eyes locked. We saw each other. And did our faces wear that wash of recognition, that sense of being hurtled backwards through time? I doubt it. The underground is not the place to wear one's heart on one's sleeve. It's the place, more than that, it's the very soul of cultivated anonymity. In which, we sink from ourselves, suspended, in blessed transition. Forever between stops. Forever elsewhere.

But whether it all came back with a bang I can't say. On some unconscious level yes it did. That was the little window opening. The information had been received. But had I understood it? Not yet. Intuitively there was more than a sense of recognition though. It was the last piece of the jigsaw, and I hadn't even known I'd been trying to stick it together. I hadn't even known the jigsaw existed.

Music. So often the passport to times past. Less so now, perhaps, when radios are forever belting out those golden oldies. And worse, those new revamped versions where they always strangle the sound and murder the tempo. To say nothing about desecrating sacred memories...or profane.

There is music in the background but I can't place it. Of course. It was Spanish, and later it would have been French. And as I think of what I did I'm amazed at my audacity. The sheer nerve of it. And so bloody thoughtless. So selfish. I didn't behave like that, did I?

And if I've repressed it, the memory of it, did Jed repress it too? Did I misinterpret it? Was there really anything strong enough to need repressing in the first place? Anyway, should it have mattered? I was rescued, wasn't I? But it was Tomlinson I'd put through the worst. He was in charge of us, poor bugger. And Miss Jones, God love her. She stayed behind. In the hope I'd turn up. And Tomlinson took the rest of the party back, on his own, hoping to God I hadn't started a trend, and that they didn't all start drifting off and disappearing.

SCHOOLBOY'S LOST WEEKS * MYSTERY OF MEMORY BOY'S RETURN.

After five weeks missing on the continent runaway schoolboy James Kelly, 16, was reunited with his parents at Heathrow yesterday. After a massive search by Spanish and French police, James, last seen at San Sebastian in August, was found wandering in the fashionable coastal region of Les Sables d'Olonne. Unable to account for his movements over the last five weeks, James, who was involved in a sea-bathing incident with his school party, during which he was nearly drowned, is thought to be suffering from amnesia. He is otherwise unharmed, but according to his mother, has lost more than a stone and a half in weight and acquired a film-star tan. 'I hardly recognised him,' a tearful Mrs Kelly told reporters. 'I'm just so glad he's alive.'

Amnesia? That seemed the safest bet....

When I got off the train, the unspectacular streets of Brockley were so safely, so reassuringly, home. And I kissed Carolyn with unaccustomed gusto, hugging the kids as if I hadn't seen them for years, as if I'd come back from a polar expedition or something, not the usual commonplace day at the office. Not that I actually work in an office as such, but never mind. Suddenly, stabbingly, I knew just what the tearful Mrs Kelly felt, reunited with her lost child that day, all of twenty five years ago. And the stiff upper lip moist eyed Mr Kelly too. Poor Dad. I'm sorry. But d'you know, it's quite crazy, it's only now, today, Dad, and I can't tell you now, even if I wanted to, even if it would help, which it wouldn't after all this time, just today, after seeing Jed like that, just a glimpse of him, just a fluke after all, that I'm beginning to really understand what happened.

I took the kids to the park, pushing Sally along on her new bike. No, not yet Daddy, I want my stabilisers on just a little bit longer. And I promise Paul a game with his new football. Yes. Of course. And you can't imagine how much this means to me, really.

Hilly Fields Park. Your funny, homely name is sweet as honey. Is magic.

I watched the coach leave. I could see it parked at the end of the road just opposite the hotel. I had a good vantage point, here in the café, sat in the window with my black coffee and my disguise. A pair of cheap new sunglasses. Ridiculous! And no one calls them sunglasses now, do they. Even Paul sports his shades and thinks himself so cool! And he's eight, for heaven's sake.

And I look down at him as he races over the grass. Don't ever do what I did, Paul, all those years ago. Don't treat me the way I treated my parents, will you?

And it wasn't as if they were in any way to blame.

Jed. What a strange thing is hero worship. And how I worshipped him. That he was my friend at all was a miracle. I blessed the ground he walked on. I dressed like him, talked like him. He was John Lennon and Mick Jagger rolled into one. And even when I had my eye on some girl, like Helen Waterhouse or Merle Morgan, and she was really something, it wasn't the same as my total involvement with Jed. Almost total. The girls were there. In the background. But in everything I did, I deferred to Jed. You'd have thought he'd get sick of it. But no. Seemed his capacity for being worshipped quite matched mine for uncritical adulation. And I wasn't alone. He could've had a gang if he'd wanted to. He didn't need one. He had the frank admiration of the rest of the lads. And he had me, whose devotion knew no bounds.

So that was why it hurt so much. That day in the sea. And why I couldn't face the truth of it. And why I flipped (now there's a term that didn't exist in the sixties. Strange really since most of us were about to flip, were in mid flip, or just recovering from the most recent flip most of the time). I couldn't face going home. I couldn't face school. I couldn't face life after this.

Could I?

But after the coach finally pulled away I saw her standing ~ there under the trees, Miss Jones. And I realised. And I think right there and then I'd have been on that coach with the rest of them if I'd felt it wasn't already too late. There was no going back. Not now. The die was cast. Priority was to keep away from the hotel, away from the eagle eyes of Miss Jones. Priority was to keep walking. And there I was with this heavy, ugly, old-fashioned suitcase. It looked all wrong. As soon as I could I'd have to dispose of it. Part exchange for a rucksack? I still had quite a bit of money. That's right, on some level I'd planned this for days. But it was only within an hour or so of the time for leaving that the plans all fell into place.

It seemed sensible to go back to Lourdes. That's where we'd spent the first six days of the holiday. We'd been there on Good Friday, watching the candlelit procession wind its way through the streets to the grotto, like a ribbon of light. By getting up to the citadel above the straggle of streets I could look down on it all, proud that I'd passed through customs with no problem, proved my independence. I didn't need Jed. I didn't need Tomlinson and a whole host of silly kids. I was free. In this strange country where no one knew me I could take stock. My school French was ropey but adequate. I could manage. I slept at the citadel that first night. It was warm and still. I woke at first light, saw a lizard scuttle off through the dusty leaves. The sky was hazy, the shimmering blue of it hidden behind an opaque glare. I needed a wash, thought back to the fountains of San Sebastian, their alternately plunging and towering plumes of water. The ilex trees were stiff sentinels. I left the citadel, moved down through the narrow streets with their striped awnings, the souvenir shops bulging with plaster saints and garish medallions, candles and incense. It was all unreal. Unreal and delightful.

Next stop Biarritz.

For the first time I thought of Jed. What did he feel when I didn't turn up at the coach? When a search of the room I shared with him and David Platt, who snored all the time, showed I'd taken my clothes from the wardrobe? The drawers were empty. I'd definitely gone. And I'd planned to go. Had I done this to hurt him? Did I succeed?

Biarritz meant long white vistas of hotels like wedding cakes, rows of palm trees, the long soft swish of the waves....

Souviens-toi....

The purring repetitive words of the song...running out of money now, getting nervous, wondering if I'd got the nerve to steal. Thinking of home in a distant, half-hearted way. I had to eat, didn't I? Then, outside one of the larger hotels, large but a little shabby perhaps, red and white flags hanging listless on their poles in the heavy air, white paint peeling ever so slightly, there was a woman sitting on one of those ornate chairs, sipping at something cool in a long stemmed glass. It was every teenager's fantasy. The older woman, sophisticated, polished, cosmopolitan. Did I see myself as some sort of baby gigolo? How ludicrous! The expression 'toy boy' didn't exist then but I suppose the phenomenon did. She would initiate me into the joys of sex. She would whisk me way to Nice, to Cannes. To Monte Carlo. We'd become inseparable. She'd buy me a casino, a race horse, an Alfa Romeo.

What she actually did was feed me, buy me a change of clothes and allow me to soak away the stain and strain of the road in a palatial if somewhat tawdry bathroom. With a bidet! But she also asked me questions, subtle questions which I thought I'd fended off with aplomb. I was kidding myself. After two days her husband appeared, a squat, and to me utterly prosaic man with dark hairs sprouting from his notrils. 'Meet our English runaway,' she greeted him, and I knew my time was up. Madame Letheule, where are you? Ignorant, arrogant, insufferable monster that I was...I owe you....

I knew the police must be on to me by now. I assumed, of course, that there was a search for me. Again, so egocentric. What sort of game did I think I was playing? Whatever it was I started to play with some expertise. I was learning. I moved inland, kept to the backroads, stole fruit and bread rolls at open markets, slept in woods at the edge of villages, was always on the move before break of day. Then the weather changed. Storms, sheet lightning, and torrential rain turned dusty tracks to sloughs of clogging mud. I got a lift in a lorry carrying a load of sheep to slaughter. I'll never forget that night, their endless bleating, their smell. From then on something was different. I became increasingly apprehensive, thought people were watching me, which, I suppose, they were. My photograph had appeared on TV, in the papers. I felt as if a net was closing in on me. I moved back to the coast. Walked through endless sandy and sunscorched pinewoods, the sea below me, the occasional sumptuous villa revealing itself in a clearing. Here there were swimming pools and terraces. Hunger made me daring. I took to helping myself at luncheons, sprinting down from the trees and escaping with cold meat, pieces of chicken, even, once, a bottle of white wine. Again it grew almost unbearably hot. My shoes had fallen to bits so I walked barefoot, avoiding the melted tar of the roads when I could.

Then I met Tanya. Another runaway. She was as wild and wary as a cat. Not French at all, but Belgian. Her father, who she'd never seen, was Russian, she said. She was a housebreaker. Astute, an adept liar. Survival was her middle name and in the five or six days we spent together I turned all my thwarted capacity for worship on to her. Unlike Jed, she did find it cloying. Her attitude, though, was enjoy it while it lasts, with more than a dash of healthy scepticism. She got us into a superb beach villa, called Knossos. I remember tiled floors of black and white marble, simple heavy furniture in dark wood, paintings of flowers and birds. Tanya raided the freezer and prepared a meal fit for a prince and a princess. That's what we were. Living in a fairy tale. So far she'd rebuffed all my awkward kisses but tonight we made love. Three times. Each time more splendid than before. And when I woke in the morning she brought me peaches and coffee. And told me to phone.

'Phone?' I said incredulously. I listened to my voice, so small and insignificant in the tall room. 'But....'

'No buts. You must. Summer's going to end soon. Can't you feel it? There's a chill in the air at night now. There's a phone here. Use it. You'll have to wait for a line. Tell your parents you're safe, but don't tell them where you are. Say you'll walk into the main police station in Nantes in two days time. That's Thursday. Do it Jimmy.'

Not only adoration. Obedience too. I did exactly what she told me, but didn't get as far as Nantes. I was picked up on the beach about thirty miles north. Tanya, meanwhile, had made herself scarce. Had told me she planned to head for Paris for the winter.

Back home I was treated with kid gloves. That made me feel bad, such a fraud. Amnesia? No way, but one thing I had forgotten, and one thing only. Seeing his face today, in the train brought it back. The same expression. Had that been the trigger? That look on Jed's face as we struggled in the sea. That look of contempt, that swivelling sideways look. I was rescued. Two young Spaniards with the musculature of Charles Atlas. I refused to look at Jed, who'd finally managed to reach the harbour steps. In the few remaining days before our planned departure, despite feeble attempts at conversation on his part, I refused to speak to him.

And never did. It caused a few raised eyebrows. Tomlinson, who was more perceptive than his hearty exterior implied, knew something was up.

'What is it with you and Humphreys, eh? You used to be thick as thieves.'

I said nothing. The mystery of my missing five weeks was very useful. My vulnerability. I capitalised on it shamelessly.

There were so many secrets. Tanya, my daughter, the child of my first, foolish marriage. Only I know the significance of the name. I think of Knossos, my sojourn with the generous and trusting Madame Letheule. I think of the sleepy, dusty villages, the vineyards, Lourdes and its citadel, the great basilica, the lizard and the ilex trees.

And that look on Jed's face. Had I seen it? Was it really there? All that malevolence.... It was a look of pure loathing. I remember the waves, choppy, grey, the insidious dragging pull of them. My mouth open, catching their foul salt clout. The sense, somehow, of not caring whether I vanished into the swell of the sea, but that passive acceptance underpinned all the time by panic, by helplessness. Had I been trying to compete with him, in swimming out so fast, so far? He'd not been that far behind, but he'd understood before I did what those whistles meant. That this place was dangerous. That no one swam here. I saw him toss his head, plunge back, away from me. The swerve of his shoulder. If I drowned, so what. It was every man for himself, wasn't it?

The look on his face.... Well, imagined or real, it changed me, changed everything, that sense of total rejection. Perhaps, after all, I owed him. He taught me a sharp, vicious lesson. Those missing weeks that followed. Missing as far as everyone else was concerned but perenially clear to me.

Had I, in reality, rejected him? To escape him, to escape the slavish part of myself. To become what I had to be.

Separate.

Shining Stones

Is my son still alive?

Remember how he said he was practising for life in a cardboard box? Folded from the rain....

Then you, Julia. Solvent abuse is just a debased form of aromatherapy. We set out, you with your squeezy bottle of sweet orange body oil. We found him in the garden of the old hospital in Sisson Street. Remember hospitals? Take off your shirt, you said. Colin lay face down on the parched grass. You kneaded his shoulders as if they were lumps of dough. He shone quietly. The oil and its pungency. How long ago? Three years? Four?

Are you still alive, Colin?

The claims they make grow more inflated all the time. A REVIVED BRITAIN LEADS THE WORLD. Of course only parts have been revived. Much remains to be done. Jump on the Zeitgeist. Move with the times.

The last time I was in London I walked with Sarah in early January drizzle across the Hungerford Bridge. The river swelled grey green, slopped in its enormous light slid bucket. At Waterloo Bridge they were waiting with their small smudged leaflets. (Where were the C.E.A.?) One of them, a gaunt boy in a long coat pushed the leaflet into my hand.

You can only effect change from within. That is the only place where change can start. You can no longer even pretend to put your faith in external mechanisms of any kind. Schemes. Systems. Structures. Of the left. Of the right. Of the middle. Forget them. Everything imposed from outside will be smashed from outside to be replaced by another form of imposition. Abstract yourself from all of these.

Sarah was contemptuous. 'It's become the fashion,' she said. 'Like sleeping in the street.'

So little comprehension, here, in the middle of it she could not see. Or would not. Where had she gone, the old real Sarah? But this new person was real too.

Goodbye Sarah, erstwhile friend.

Our names are on their computers. It's just a matter of time.

The Cost Effectiveness Assessors move in straight lines. They will flush us out. The C.E.A. The beaters. Like grouse out of the heather. They have their maps. They have their lists of names. The roadblocks are highly efficient. So easy, you'd think they'd be embarassed.

We're remote here at Pen y Gadair. A breathing space. That's all.

We got them from the river bottom. We carried them up to the house. In boxes. In plastic carrier bags. The shining stones. We piled them round the doors, round the windows, ready and waiting for when they come.

We have remained true to what we are. Absurd. Outmoded. Risible. Quaint, I suppose, believing as we do that, ultimately, physical survival is not the most important thing. We decided that long ago.

I remember that last look on Sarah's face.

'You're antediluvian,' she said. 'That's what you are. Neolithic.' So?

Technocrats and Servitors. All that are left. And how do we fit in?

We can't be categorised. That's why they have to kill us. It does make sense.

I love the earth, the light on the mountain, the berries on our rowan tree. I love you, all of you. Danny, Simeon, Krishna, Lerry, Ma Leghorn, Julia, Raj, Luma, Glyn.

And every day my aim is improving.

I love my heaps of shining stones.

Acknowledgements

Some of these stories have appeared in *Planet* and *The New Welsh Review*. 'Scream, Scream' appeared in *The Green Bridge: Stories from Wales*, edited by John Davies (Seren Books), and was broadcast on Radio 4.

This books was written with the assistance of a bursary from the Welsh Arts Council.